CURVES AND BENDS AND CARS
THAT WON'T COME FAST

CURVES AND BENDS AND CARS THAT WON'T COME FAST

BRIAN FLEMING

PHOENIX HOUSE
London

First published in Great Britain in 1999
by Phoenix House

© 1999 Brian Fleming
The moral right of Brian Fleming to be
identified as the author of this work
has been asserted in accordance with
the Copyright, Designs and Patents Act of 1988.

A CIP catalogue record for this book is
available from the British Library.

ISBN 1 861591 25 X (cased)
     1 861591 28 4 (paperback)

Typeset at The Spartan Press Ltd
Lymington, Hants

Set in Minion

Printed in Great Britain by
Clays Ltd, St Ives plc

Phoenix House

Weidenfeld & Nicolson
The Orion Publishing Group Ltd
Orion House
5 Upper Saint Martin's Lane
London WC2H 9EA

Contents

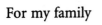

For my family

Part One
A VAGUE SENSE OF DELIVERANCE

Playing

As kids we used to spend our summer vacations on a small, isolated lake in Vermont's Green Mountains. For the most part we had the lake to ourselves. Only a few other houses dotted the shore in those days, each nestled into its own private cove hidden from view by surrounding forest. I could imagine, as I paddled our canoe the length of the lake, dipping the paddle from side to side in fluid, easy motions I was proud of, that I was the only human alive in the world. I imagined myself living in a wigwam on the lake's shore, in the mornings fishing for my breakfast as the mist pulled off the water, in the evenings sitting by my fire staring up at an eagle floating on the air high above this earth. Skimming across the water like that, the lake was beautiful to me. It was when I stopped and bent my head over the side close to the water and tried to pierce the shimmer of sunlight that illuminated the surface that I became scared, filled with dark thoughts of what creatures might lurk below.

At the top end of the lake where it tapered into a stream, the water was clear and you could see right through to the shallow bottom. Just past the mouth of the stream a pool had formed, backed up against a logjam. At the bottom of the pool there rested a sunken row boat, its wood soft from rot and algae, with planks missing from its hull and a tear on its underside. I imagined the boat to be hundreds of years old, manned by white explorers who had tried to take their skiff upstream when the stream had still been a river, before being ambushed by a band of Iroquois lying in wait in the underbrush. Bronze warriors in loincloths, with vivid paints smearing their bodies and their scalps shaved into mohawks. That's how I imagined them, unleashing their spears and arrows and axes on the white men, leaving their bodies stripped naked of gear and clothes. I would search for any remains of the boatmen or evidence of the raid, but all I ever found were stones, worn flat by water, that could be mistaken for arrowheads. These I collected in my canoe only to later toss away.

Past the logjam the stream lost itself in a tangle of branches and fallen trees. Once or twice I left the canoe and climbed the jam, making my way over the slippery rocks deeper into the forest, the lake disappearing behind me, closed off by the dense plant life the sunlight couldn't penetrate. But I never went far, frightened by the silence and the enclosing vegetation, and I always wondered what lay further upstream.

The lake was surrounded on three sides by forested hills and on the fourth by a low, craggy mountain with a broad cliff cut from its face in the shape of an eagle with its wings splayed and head snapped to the side. It was from this the mountain drew its name: Eagle Rock. I always dreamed of standing atop that mountain, but our dad couldn't hike because of a war injury, and my sister Anna and our mom had no interest. I was too scared to go on my own. Our cottage sat just off the water across the lake from Eagle Rock and on clear days with no wind to ruffle the surface of the water, I'd stare at the reflection of the mountain and compare it to the real thing, trying to discover the difference.

Anna, twelve and a year older than I was, our cousin Veronica, thirteen, and I lived in the basement of the cottage where our parents never bothered us much except to call us to meals from the top of the stairs. I couldn't know this then, but they were embroiled in their own world of financial difficulties and attendant marital problems and this would be the last summer we spent on the lake.

Usually the three of us woke early only to waste the morning in bed talking, though it was mostly Anna and Veronica who did the talking, while I, the younger brother and cousin, only listened. We shared a room with two bunk beds. I had a top bunk and Anna and Veronica the beds below. They would huddle together in the one beneath my bunk where I couldn't see them and whisper among themselves. I'd flip through my favourite comic book without reading the captions while trying to catch a hint of what they were saying. If it was whispered, it had to be important.

Sometimes I could hear Veronica say my name and could hear them giggle, and sometimes Anna would ask if I wanted to climb into bed with them, but I never did. When she didn't ask, I'd pretend not to care.

On warm days we swam and lay out on the raft. At Veronica's urging, she and Anna would lie out in only their bikini bottoms, uncaring of who might see. Veronica made a show of it: reach around slowly to unclasp the top, or else ask me to do it; draw the useless bit of cloth away from her body; arch her back as she lay down. Anna just took the thing off the way she might take off her coat. It was things like this that made her seem more than just a year older. My friends at school all said she was beautiful. They couldn't believe it when I told them she was twelve; she was the kind of girl who looked more experienced than you could ever dream, they said, who in grade school had a boyfriend at the local high school and in high school would have a boyfriend in college and in college would be courted by the sons of oil barons and after college by celebrities, if she didn't become one herself.

Anna's breasts were mere humps that disappeared when she lay flat, with small and boy-like nipples – like my own – and it was only in the last year her waist and hips had taken on curves mine didn't have. But she was my sister and it was Veronica, that summer, with full, fleshy breasts and wide hips, who made me afraid and queasy when she got near and left me out of breath when she went away. Lying on that raft, I would peek out of the corner of my eye to catch sight of her tanned body, with round nipples twice the size of mine topping the mounds of her boobs and a wave-like shape when she lay on her side and a look on her face that made me want to run before it could capture me. I couldn't help myself; I wanted to roll my body next to hers and feel her against me and touch her skin. Sometimes she caught me looking and held my gaze, smiling, and I would want to disappear. Other times she'd ask me to rub her with lotion – a task that made me shake – directing where I should place my hands. Or else she'd touch her breasts when she thought

I was looking. Or adjust her bikini bottom. To her it was a game.

Anna would lie there, her eyes closed in the sun. But sometimes I'd spy her. She'd open her eyes a peek to watch Veronica. I would look away then, afraid my sister might see into me and see there the thoughts I had of Veronica. Thoughts that became more and more vivid.

There was a day that summer I took the canoe out to the middle of the lake where no one could see me, and swam naked in the water. I liked being there alone and liked the water cold and clean between my legs. As long as I didn't think of the darkness beneath me, I was all right. As long as I thought only of the sensation of water.

I was a good swimmer, and strong, but when I saw that the current had swept the canoe some hundred feet uplake, tugging it gently towards the stream at the top, all my fears welled up of what unseen monsters – giant garfish, fresh-water kraken, man-eating seaweed – might lie beneath me in the darkness of the lake. I went cold thinking of myself alone at the centre of the lake, only my head bobbing above the surface. I began to kick and flail and thrash to stay afloat, to keep away anything that might attack from below. My heart thumped in my chest. I held a scream tight inside my lungs, unwilling to unleash it, but it came out anyway.

'Anna, Anna.' I'd never liked relying on my sister, or anyone, for help, but in my panic I didn't care. I wanted only to be out of the water, on solid ground. 'Anna. Veronica. Anna.' Through the sounds of my thrashing I heard my voice bounce off the hills and come back to me.

The more I called, the more it came back. It didn't sound like mine any more.

I kicked to get my head as far above the surface as possible and shouted their names again. On the dock I saw them ready the *Sunfish* sailboat and began to feel safer. Tentatively I calmed my flailing, still nervous of what might lurk below. I wished I hadn't cried out to them and let them see my fear, but I was relieved they were on their way. When they came within reach, though, they sailed past me. Anna looked like she was ready to reach out a hand, but Veronica, who manned the *Sunfish*, was laughing. She began to circle me.

'Anna,' I pleaded. 'Anna, please.'

Anna yelled at Veronica to stop the boat. 'Are you all right? I thought you were drowning.' She held out her hand, but I refused to take it.

'I got a cramp. My leg cramped. It's nothing.'

'Don't yell like that, Paul, if you don't mean it. I'm serious. Don't do that to me. The next time you yell we might not come.'

Veronica laughed. 'You should've heard yourself scream.'

'I did mean it. My leg cramped, I'm serious. It's not funny.' But I had heard myself scream, had heard the echo from off the mountain.

'Where are your trunks?' Veronica asked. She was looking through the water at my pale middle. She smiled and suddenly I wished I'd been left to the mercies of the deep. I kicked my legs to disguise my nakedness, but felt my face burn.

'What did you do with your bathing suit, Paul?' Anna asked.

'I had to pee.'

'You don't need to take your trunks off to do that,' Veronica pointed out. On this occasion I hadn't actually been getting myself off, but I began to wonder if she knew what I did lying on my stomach in my bunk all night or why I spent so much time in the bathroom.

'Your face is all red,' Anna said. 'You should get in the boat before you explode.'

'Leave me alone.'

'They're in the canoe, I bet,' Veronica said. 'We should go get them.' She pulled the mainsheet in tight to catch the wind, but I grabbed at the hull and lifted my chest onto the slick plexiglas surface.

'Look how white his butt is,' Veronica laughed.

'You're going to have to come all the way in if we're going to get anywhere,' Anna said. Then she said, 'What were you doing out here?'

'I wasn't doing anything.'

Without looking at either of them, I pulled myself onto the hull and slithered to the bow where I lay on my stomach with my legs closed and my arms dangling over the sides. I tried to put their presence out of my mind and focus on the point where the boat parted the water in two, but behind me I could hear Veronica whisper something to Anna.

Before we got to the canoe, Anna slid up beside me. She touched my back; I pulled away as best I could. 'It's OK, Paul,' she said.

'Don't touch me.'

'I wasn't laughing at you.'

On the days it rained the lake's surface looked like it

swarmed with a million insects. Across the way Eagle Rock disappeared in a shroud of mist and clouds. I felt transported to a different world where there was no access road, no cars to be heard racing by, no sounds of oars on the lake or the sight of other people or houses. On days like this we stayed inside in the basement wearing only our pyjamas or underwear, a fire crackling in the fireplace.

We played a game which involved one of us lying on his or her stomach with their shirt pulled up while another of us would use their fingers to write or draw on the person's bare back. The person on their stomach would have to guess what had been written or drawn on their back. It was always either Veronica and Anna who played, or me and Veronica. Whenever Anna wanted to draw on my back, I lied and said I didn't feel like playing. When she wanted me to draw on hers, which happened more often, I made some feeble attempts before giving up, ignoring her encouragements and turning to a comic book.

'At least try, Paul. You can't just give up,' she'd say.

'I don't want to.'

'That's no way to go through life. You have to do things.'

'I don't want to.' But that was a lie.

Veronica: I loved the weight of her on me as she drew. Loved the feel of her fingers brushing across my skin and not being able to see her, lost in the sensation. Loved her body so close to mine and the attention she gave to what she was doing. My favourite was when she erased what she'd drawn by making slow, broad squiggly lines across my back from shoulder blade to shoulder blade, then down my spine to the small of my back, and started over. When it was my turn, though, I became nervous and never knew what to do.

All I wanted was to lean my chest against her back to take in her warmth, but she would tap her shoulder with her finger and say, 'Draw.'

Another game we played was the tickle game. In the tickle game you had to lie still on your back, blindfolded, while the other person tried to get you to laugh by touching lightly in places like the pits of your arms, on the inside of your elbow, below your ribcage, in the crook of your thigh, around and behind your knee. They weren't allowed to tickle you outright, just to touch. It was a contest of wills, to see who could last the longest without giving in to laughter. Veronica, who had introduced this game that summer, always preferred to be the one doing the touching. A sly grin on her face, she could do it with torturous patience, confident her teasing caress would have the desired effect, but I refused to laugh no matter how much it hurt. When it was my turn to tickle her I couldn't stand the idea of such sensuous touch and soon went overboard, bringing her to laughter and losing the game.

Anna didn't care about winning or losing; she let the giggles come over her and even gave instructions on how and where to touch her. She wanted to do the same to me and would tell me I just needed to let go, but I wouldn't allow her and always tore off my blindfold.

'Do you not like me?' she asked me after I threw one of these fits.

'You're my sister,' I replied as if that would cover both possible responses.

'Then why are you such a shit? We don't have to include you, you know. We're doing you a favour.'

'I'm telling Mom what you just said. Shit.'

'No, you're not. Besides, she doesn't care anyway.'

'Does, too.'

Of course I didn't tell our mother anything and eventually returned to join Anna and Veronica in their games. It was Veronica's turn to touch me and she told me to stretch my arms over my head. It was a dare, because it would leave my underarms exposed, but I was up to the challenge, sure that I could stifle my laughter. I felt her weight settle on my thighs. It was trick to make me feel more in her control and less able to hold back my giggles. Also, she knew how claustrophobic I was. Panic was my usual response when I couldn't move or see, but since that day on the lake I'd resolved not to let fear overwhelm and embarrass me again. It took everything I had not to begin thrashing, pinned and blindfolded as I was. But then I felt another weight settle on my arms, which could only be Anna.

'Unfair,' I called out.

There came no response. Instead I felt two sets of hands on me. Caressing the pits of my arms and the tender inside of my forearms, my ribcage, my abdomen and belly button, my hips, the inside of my thighs. I wore only a pair of tighty-whities and was sure they could see my pecker pressing against the fabric.

'Stop it,' I yelled. 'Stop.'

A hand clamped itself around my shrunken scrotum, squeezing. I jumped, could hear them giggle, and wondered who was touching me where. I twisted my hips, tried to kick free and wrench my arms away, but was pinned. I tried again, uselessly. Tried to at least get the blindfold off. Nothing. They had me, and I could sense a wail building inside me, the wail I'd sworn to stifle. Against my will, my pecker stiffened some more.

'Look,' I heard Veronica say from her place on my thighs.

'Let me go,' I screamed.

The wail came loose inside me. I began to thrash wildly, using all my little strength, jerking my knees, kicking. I got first one, then another leg free, followed by my arms. I didn't care if I hit or hurt, lost in a frenzy of wild body parts. Finally I got my blindfold off and ran into the bunk room and slammed the door behind me. There I crawled into my bed. I wrapped myself in my blankets. My body was warm. I lay on my stomach and squirmed against the mattress until the comfort and warmth left me in a hot rush. Afterwards I felt weak and lonely, disgusted at myself for needing that sensation. Disgusted that the lake and the woods and the hills, my excursions up the creek, my flights of fantasy, weren't enough. That there was more, and that it could make me feel so helpless.

In bed at night, while Anna and Veronica slept, the room dark except for the pale glow of the night-light in the corner, there were times I became frightened of the dark. It was the same fear that took hold when I swam alone in the water. The fear that something was going to swallow me whole. That I would disappear without trace. On nights like this I would whisper Anna's name to see if she was awake.

'Anna,' I whispered. 'Anna.'

'Yeah,' she groaned from her half-sleep.

'What do you think death is like?'

'Death?'

'Yeah.'

'I think it's a place where we go where no one ever dies and when we get there this will all be just a dream. We're living a dream. When we wake up we'll be in Heaven. Then we fall back asleep and have another dream. We're all dreams.'

'I think it's kind of like the lake,' I said, 'except without the houses and cars and it's never cold and no one wears any clothes and everyone lives in the woods or on the water and doesn't have to do anything except play and eat fruit and swim and run and there's nothing to be scared of.' But this wasn't completely true. This was just the way I wanted death to be. I had an inkling, even then, at the age of eleven, that death was otherwise. That it was an erasure of existence. Over, done.

'Are you scared?' Anna asked.

'Sometimes.'

'Are you scared now?'

'Not any more,' I lied.

'I think Heaven is a place where everyone is waiting for you. It's where we'll all be together again,' Veronica said. I twitched, embarrassed that she'd heard what we'd been talking about. I didn't want for her to know this side of me. I had an image of myself as a person without fear who could not be controlled or touched by the world.

For a long while we lay in silence. I was afraid Veronica and Anna had fallen asleep, but didn't want to whisper their names again.

'It's hot,' Veronica finally said. 'I'm taking my undies off.' I peeked over my bunk to see her drop something to the floor. 'I love being naked in bed. We should all get naked. Just like we're in Heaven.'

Anna shuffled in the bunk below me. 'It feels nice,' she said.

'Are you naked, Paul?' Veronica asked.

I stayed quiet for a moment, then said, 'Yeah,' even though I still wore my underwear. I heard Veronica throw the sheet from her bed and looked over. She lay on her back with her hands on her stomach, but in the shallow green light of the room I could barely see her. It made me want to lie alone beside her, and I took my tighty-whities off and pushed my own blanket aside. I rubbed myself, then stopped, afraid Veronica might see; then started again, hoping she would.

'Is it nice swimming naked?' Anna asked from below.

I didn't answer at first, caught with my hand on my pud. Then I said, 'Yeah.' It felt strange making this admission to my sister, but the dark made it easier.

'We should go,' Veronica said. 'Your parents are asleep. Let's sneak out of the house and swim out to the raft.' She stood without waiting for a response. Below me I could hear Anna join her. I didn't want to be left alone in the room and I sat up, but waited for them to walk past before I climbed out.

Outside the air was warm. We stood on the end of the deck and I could feel my penis sticking finger-like into the air, tickled by the breeze. No one said anything – we just looked at the stars strewn across the sky. All three of us. It was like in my fantasies of this place, like my vision of Heaven. I didn't even mind Anna being there, didn't mind that if she turned around and looked down she'd see my happy erection.

One by one we climbed into the water, Veronica first, then Anna, then me. I was the best swimmer and beat them to the raft, but instead of climbing onto it, I continued on until I could barely make out the raft from the dark.

'Where are you, Paul? Are you all right?' I heard Anna whisper.

I didn't answer and let myself sink below the surface. When I opened my eyes everything was black around me with no top or bottom or up or down; it was all the same, above and below, outside and inside – all the same blackness. My only fear was of hitting bottom, so I kicked myself up again and, breaking the surface, gulped in a lung full of air.

'Paul?' I heard my name again.

'I'm here.'

'Don't do that,' Anna said. 'Come sit on the raft with us and look at the sky.'

I returned to the raft where she and Veronica lay on their backs with their hands folded behind their heads. 'I was all right,' I said without any of the indignation I normally felt when Anna mothered me. I stayed in the water, circling the raft. From where I was I could easily see Veronica. She looked different from Anna, different than I expected, with a small dark patch between her legs that Anna didn't have. I began to rub at myself, letting the warmth come. I liked that Anna and Veronica had no idea what I was doing. Liked that I was hidden in the dark like this and was unafraid.

'I kissed a boy at school,' Veronica said into the air.

'Only one?' Anna asked.

'No. But this one I really kissed. With our mouths open.'

'That's gross,' I said from the water. Kissing still seemed
to me the frivolous, useless act of adults.

'No it's not; it's great. I didn't want to stop. You'll get to
like it.'

'No I won't.'

'I kissed one boy, but didn't like it,' Anna said in the
matter-of-fact way she approached all experiences of the
world.

Eventually I grew cold and swam for the deck. Behind me
I heard Anna and Veronica dive into the water.

Once in the basement, we built a fire. All three of us still
naked, we huddled under one blanket before it, surrounded
by skin and warmth. I didn't know who touched me where
and didn't care. It was like floating in the black water. No up
and down. No fear. Veronica lay pressed against my back
and I felt the brush of soft hair on my thigh. I tried to draw
away from Anna, who had her back to me, but there wasn't
any room and the warmth was nice. Permanent.

'Does that feel good?' asked Anna.

'What?'

'When your thingy's like that.'

'What's his thingy doing?' Veronica asked, propping
herself on an elbow.

'It's not doing anything,' I snapped, but I was aroused by
her.

'Can I touch it?' asked Anna. She rolled to face me.

'Yeah, I want to touch it.' Veronica pulled away the
blanket.

'No,' I said and stood up. I sat down in front of the fire
with my back to them. My face stung from the heat. My

pecker was full hard and I didn't want them to see me like this. Under the blanket, in the blackness, it was fine, still my secret, but out in the open I felt I was giving myself up – that they were taking from me a part I didn't want them to have.

'Can you make it do that?' Anna asked.

I didn't answer.

'I would hate to be a boy,' Veronica said. 'I love being a girl. All boys want is girls, but girls want everything.'

'Will you lie down with us again, Paul?' Anna asked.

'No.'

'Please. Come lie back down.'

'No.'

Anna didn't say anything more. Silence settled. I missed the warmth of the blanket, missed that feeling of oblivion, of sensation, but I was too proud to return to the comfort they offered.

I looked over my shoulder and saw that Veronica and Anna had fallen asleep. I shuffled over to them and lifted the blanket aside. Before crawling under, I looked at Veronica. I tried first to memorize all of her body, then gave in to the falling sensation inside me.

I lay down next to her. After a moment, I put my arm around her. I wanted to wake her.

'Veronica,' I whispered. 'Are you awake?' Beside her I heard Anna sigh in her sleep.

Veronica didn't stir and I tried again. Finally, she said, 'Yeah.'

'It's like that,' I said.

'What is?'

'You know.'

She turned to face me.

'Do you want to touch it?' I asked. 'You can, if you want.'

'Are you sure?'

'Yeah.'

It took her a moment. When she touched my erect penis, I shook. Her fingers were hot. I closed my eyes.

'Is this what you do?' Veronica began moving her hand in a way that felt a million times better than I'd ever made myself feel. 'This is funny.' She giggled, then said, 'I want you to hump me.' She rolled onto her back and pulled me on top of her. I knew enough about the way adults had sex to imitate it, and I moved my hips in circles the way I did against my mattress or a pillow when I was alone. Her skin was hot and the hair between her legs coarse.

'It feels funny,' she giggled. 'It tickles.'

Next to us I saw that Anna was awake. She was watching, but I didn't care. I didn't want to stop.

'Paul, you're tickling me,' Veronica laughed beneath me. 'Stop.' She tried to push me from her. 'Stop.'

'Here,' Anna said and tugged on my arm. She lay on her back with her legs open and pulled me on top of her. She sighed and giggled and said, 'You're warm,' and I pushed against her not knowing what I was doing or why, pushing and pushing, thinking that all I had to do was push, and she asked, 'Does it feel nice?' and then it was like a pop and Anna gave out a sharp yelp and I felt like I was sliding and falling and floating all at the same time. I began to jerk, not knowing any more what was happening, what I was feeling.

'You look funny,' I heard Veronica say. Then I heard her say, 'I think you should stop.'

'What does it feel like?' Anna asked through her teeth.

She had her eyes open and clenched her jaw. She pulled air in through her nose in short spurts. 'Does it feel nice?'

'Stop it,' Veronica cried. 'Stop it. Don't.'

Whatever was driving me disappeared and fell away. I stopped and pulled myself from Anna. There was blood on the inside of her thighs and on my penis and I wanted to vomit. Veronica was crying. Anna had her eyes closed now. She looked lost and with her eyes shut and her lips slightly parted, she reached out for me, but I jerked away. I wanted to hide, to be somewhere else, and I ran for the bunk room where I climbed into my bed and wrapped the blanket around me in an attempt to rediscover that pleasant, painless darkness from before.

The next morning when Anna tried to wake me, I pretended to be asleep. She tickled me and I rolled over. It was as if nothing had happened.

'It's a great day out. No clouds,' she said. 'We should go sailing.'

'No.'

'Come on, let's go sailing.'

'Where's Veronica?'

'She's upstairs with Mom and Dad. Come on. Let's go. Just you and me.'

'No.'

I spent the rest of the morning in bed wrapped in my blanket, the curtains drawn, the windows closed. I refused to eat. In the afternoon I took the canoe out onto the lake and up to the stream where I tied it to the logjam and waded up the creek imagining I was an Indian warrior with my hair shaved into a mohawk and feathers in my ears and my face painted. I imagined myself with the face of an Indian: strong and unsmiling. Resilient. Proud. Then I imagined myself perched atop Eagle Rock in my leathers, awaiting the coming of winter and looking down on the world of the lake with only the sound of the wind through the trees around me. This I could understand. I turned around and went back to my canoe, untied it, and paddled across the lake in the direction of the shore from which Eagle Rock rose. I paddled fast and in a straight line. The water seemed to barely break beneath me.

Curves and Bends and Cars
that Won't Come Fast

When Peter was ten years old and still lived in Germany he'd wait on the concrete kerb in front of his house for cars to approach. The street stretched long and straight, and from where he crouched he could watch the cars barrel towards him between the stern, silent stares of the aged houses on either side. It didn't matter what kind of car – Mercedes, BMW, Ford, Fiat, Volkswagen. He wouldn't do anything obvious to prepare himself. He had no way of measuring when he'd run, didn't count out the car's approach or estimate its distance, but knew in his head, could feel the moment inside him. In the narrow margin of time in which it would be too late for the car to brake and in which, if he tripped or missed a stride, he might die, just as out of the corner of his eye he caught the dull reflection of light off the front fender – so close he could almost touch it – he ran, head high, torso straight, pumping with his thin boy's legs to make it across the street just feet from the passing car.

Sometimes the drivers swerved or hit the brakes or pressed on the horn. Other times they drove on as if nothing had happened. Occasionally one rolled down the window and shouted: '*Bist du bekloppt, Junge?*' What are you, brain damaged, kid?

On the other sidewalk, with the car gone, disappeared, and adrenalin slipping through his body so that he felt he was stepping on cushions of air, his hands cold, sweat like sudden condensation between his shoulder blades, along the ridge of his spine, in the hollow below his chest, his breaths coming in heaves, he'd experience a sharp stroke of disappointment. Disappointment at not having run the car closer – having, instead, held back on himself, weighed down by some sober sense of preservation that he tried to spit out onto the sidewalk.

He'd walk back and forth, cursing and filled with disgust. Then he'd take his place on the kerb, stare up the street and wait for the next car.

After Peter got to America he stopped running cars. In the town his family moved to they didn't have cinder sidewalks, or any sidewalks at all, and the road in front of the house wasn't straight, but instead a series of curves and bends and the cars didn't come fast. He took to waiting on the lawn, trying to guess when the next one would appear around the corner and sometimes, by pure luck, he'd be right.

His parents bought him a car for his sixteenth birthday, a used 81 VW Scirocco – white, low, with a standard transmission.

They lived in that part of New Hampshire where the state, otherwise landlocked, lays claim to a short stretch of the Atlantic Ocean with a determined thumb of coast. The first night Peter had the car he took it to the beach and circled the strip: the drunk and sunburned waving cans of beer from balconies; tourist shops decorated with bikinis, sunglasses, gaudy T-shirts; amusement halls rattling and ringing with the noise of a thousand video games and pinball machines that had long since left him bored. The crowds crawled the concrete boardwalk, back and forth. Cars jammed the streets, passengers called out the location of parties from inside a Camaro, a Vette, an open-sided van blasting heavy metal music. With his windows down, the radio on, Peter inched his way around the circuit, waiting for something to happen. Waiting for something to come his way.

He started doing this almost every night of the week during the summer, two, three hours around the boardwalk. At the end of the night he'd head north along route 1A, following the sea wall away from the lights. Beyond the wall the ocean lay the same colour as the night. Sometimes he'd stop to listen to the waves, or watch them break on the rocks, a swirl of black and silver in the moonlight. Other times he'd take the car up to fifty, sixty miles an hour on the winding road, feeling its weight press hard against the turns and threatening to slip away from him, working against the centrifugal tug like an angler playing a fish, then taking the next one faster, harder. At seventy-five miles an hour, as he came around the broad curve by the Rye jetties one night, the tyres caught on the tar. The car, out of his control, spun, turned and rolled – once, twice, three times, an eternity – round and round an unmoving centre, until it landed on its wheels just inches away from the salt marsh.

Peter jumped out and kicked the wheels, the mangled bumper, the door. He cursed himself. Cursed having taken the curve a touch too hard, having gone too far, over-shooting the moment of ecstasy that lay between caution and catastrophe. A state of grace. A pinnacle. The point where infinity touched and sprang away.

'Motherfuck,' he shouted. 'God damn motherfuck.'

He shook. He felt queasy. He couldn't stop moving. Only later did he think he was lucky to be alive. Think it was lucky no one else had been on that road – another car, a pedestrian. Awake in his bed at night he'd imagine their deaths on his hands and felt a hole widen within him, and he had to open his eyes to stop the falling sensation.

The next summer he bought an ounce of weed. He smoked it out of a homemade bowl and started mixing drinks from his parents' liquor cabinet before heading to the beach. The world began to feel closed around him.

In his last year of high school Peter had the use of his brother's old car. Coming home from school he hit Mill Road, a long straight stretch like the one he used to run cars on in Germany, but where the houses sat in humble security, grateful for the space they'd been allowed. He'd take the beat-up Oldsmobile up to seventy-five, seventy-six, seventy-seven before slowing to make the stop sign. He quit doing this when a man came running after him from his yard, screaming at him to slow down. In the rear-view mirror Peter saw the man tear down the street and behind the man, sitting in a pile of newly raked leaves in his yard, he saw a child, two years, three years. Old enough to walk on the road.

Peter wanted to tell the man, 'I'm sorry, I didn't see your

kid. I wasn't thinking. I'm sorry.' But he couldn't imagine loving anything as fiercely as this man did his child and was scared to face him.

The summer after he graduated from high school Peter returned to Germany for the first time in eight years. He went to his old neighbourhood, but the street looked different than he remembered and he wondered if maybe he'd dreamed everything: climbing high through the branches of the oaks in the yard; racing his bike in circles around the house; running cars.

On the autobahn at night, between Frankfurt and Wiesbaden, Peter took his father's Audi up to two hundred and twenty klicks. It had another twenty on the speedometer and could do it, but already he felt like the tyres had disappeared from underneath the body and the car was only skimming across a sheet of air. He held the speed for a minute – a Porsche, a Mercedes passed on his left – then slowed, relieved and disappointed.

Friday and Saturday nights he took the car into Sachsenhausen, the oldest part of Frankfurt where the houses hung over narrow, cobblestoned streets and you could walk from bar to bar or drink cider in an *Apfelweinstube*. He'd sit on the benches in the courtyard outside the Irish Bar, drinking Guinness, watching the Americans, the Brits, the Germans stagger past. One night he met a girl, a German, whose name he never caught. She'd just dumped her American boyfriend for making a habit of visiting the whorehouses on Kaiserstrasse. On their way out of Sachsenhausen they waited at a traffic light and sat in silence in the Audi. When the light flicked from red to yellow to green, Peter squealed the tyres and drew smoke. The girl gripped at the sides of the seat while up ahead pedestrians crossing the street went into a jog to get to the other side.

'*Muß das sein?*' she asked. Must you do this?

'*Natürlich muß es sein.*' Of course.

Peter was drunk, but pretended to be sober. The next day he couldn't remember the ride back to the apartment his parents kept in a nondescript town just outside the city limits. He did remember being with the girl in the apartment, though. They'd sat on the couch and talked, then kissed. She said he could do with her what he wanted, and in the morning she was gone. It was his first time. Paralysed by a hangover, Peter had trouble recollecting the details of what they'd done together and could find no memory of sensation. He was left with an aching desire – a desire that spread into the last recesses of his body – to feel something that would break through the numbness that had come to surround him.

Back in the States he went for an AIDS test. The doctor said he was low risk. Still, Peter's hands shook and his voice cracked when he called for the results. He gave his confidential code, then waited while the woman on the other line looked it up in the computer.

'Negative,' she said.

He was eighteen, in college. He took to driving drunk around Atlanta's winding, tree-lined suburban streets after nights at the bars or coming back from parties. He kept a twelve of Hamms under the back seat for just this purpose; he didn't care by that time of night if they were warm. In the mornings he could never remember where he'd parked. It would take him a moment and sometimes he'd have to search a number of possible locations around campus. Once, when he couldn't find his car, he was sure someone had stolen it until he saw where the gate of a parking garage had been run through. He found his car on the third deck down, bits of red and white wood stuck in its front bumper.

Peter drove fast on these late-night rides. He looked out for cops or pedestrians or other cars and talked to himself in a frustrated rage, consumed by vague notions of deliverance he'd forget by morning. Driving served to hold off the slow, steady confinement – the feeling of being locked, without means of escape, in his body. One night he drove home from a party drunk and high on Ecstasy. Stoned from smoking dope. He approached stop lights at sixty miles an hour and waited until he was within a hundred, sometimes fifty, feet of the light before hitting the brakes and letting the car skid on the rain-slicked road. A friend of his in the car that night told him about it the next day. He said he'd been sure they would die.

'Well, we're alive, aren't we?' Peter joked. But he felt scared.

On another occasion, after an afternoon of drinking and taking bong hits, he drove across Atlanta into Fulton County to buy cocaine from a fraternity acquaintance. He paid a hundred dollars and did two, three, four lines. It made him feel awake. Unbound. An inkling of the transcendence he sought. On his way back to campus, he became lost. The streets were empty, post-apocalyptic almost in the glow of the night, and the pot made them all look alike. He drove in circles – Decatur Street, Decatur Avenue; Peach

Tree this; Peach Tree that – they all had the same names. He hallucinated: thought he was back in New Hampshire on the ocean road. Thought he could hear the waves crash and scatter, hear them draw back into the dark for another go. He thought the world was different, he was different. In the morning he found himself in the parking lot of a Kroger's grocery store in a shopping centre two minutes from campus.

For a while he started going to the church on campus, but he didn't believe in God and couldn't accept anyone else being responsible for his actions. He read as much philosophy as he could, listened to music, read poetry, tried to write it, occasionally found himself having sex with one girl or another who told him he seemed so innocent. None of this could shed the sense of desolation he felt lying just beneath his skin. Not like alcohol could, or driving fast, tempting fate. Getting stoned served only to make him forget it was there.

He'd been hoping to transfer to another school but hadn't received a decision yet. Close to the end of his second semester his fraternity threw a party. Upstairs in the hallway of the fraternity house he saw one of the brothers, a senior he'd never much liked, come from a room. He was zipping up his pants and smiled at Peter. When he was gone Peter looked in the room. A girl lay passed out on the couch wearing only her bra. Her top, skirt and panties had been tossed to the floor. Something that he guessed was either vomit or semen smeared her chin and breasts. He wiped her clean and tried to wake her. He dressed her, then carried her to his car. When she finally came to, he wanted to ask what had happened, but she didn't look in any condition to know.

'Where are we going?' she asked, her words a slurred mumble. 'I don't want to leave. Take me back.'

'I'm taking you home. You need to get to sleep.' He didn't want to say more. It occurred to him he didn't know who she was or where she lived.

She tried to get out of the car, but Peter reached across and slammed the door shut, then fastened her seat belt across her waist and chest. She tried to work it open, but was too drunk. Peter gave her a beer to keep her occupied. She threw it out the window.

'Are you trying to score with me?'

'No,' Peter said. Then he said, 'I just need to know where you live. So I can drop you off.'

'Because I'm not going to sleep with you.' Peter was drunk and decided he would drive until they either found where she lived or she told him. Returning to his dorm with her wasn't an option.

As he accelerated, she grabbed the wheel. The car swung and ran up onto the sidewalk and the sudden jolt of hitting the kerb snapped Peter against his seat belt. The tyre, he knew immediately, had ruptured. The girl laughed. She held her head where she'd hit the dash. A trickle of blood was visible from below her hairline. Behind them Peter saw the red and blue lights of a cop car. He backed off the kerb and on the air still left in the other three tyres started forward. At the same time the girl undid her seat belt. She opened the door and began to step out. Peter slowed as he heard the cop shout through his microphone for them to stop.

While the cop brought his car up behind them, the girl got free of the car and walked ahead down the street. In the cruiser's spotlight Peter saw her take her top off.

'Turn off the engine and step out of the car,' the officer instructed, standing by the open door of his cruiser, the microphone in one hand, his gun in the other. 'Step out with your hands where I can see them.'

The girl moved out of the range of the spotlight, but Peter could still see she'd dropped her skirt and was naked. She was heading towards the intersection with the main campus road. The same road he barrelled down when he returned from his drunken joy rides.

'Step out of the car,' the officer repeated. 'Now.'

Peter had no reason to think anything would happen to her, no reason to think she wouldn't stop before crossing the intersection, or that anyone coming down the road wouldn't see her. He was merely following through.

'I *will* shoot,' said the officer.

Peter gunned his car forward, squealing across the tar with one flat tyre wobbling beneath him.

'Shit,' he heard the policeman say through the microphone.

The girl had made it halfway across the intersection. From the left, dropping down the hill, a car approached. As its brake lights flared Peter pressed the accelerator and ran his car across the intersection between the girl and the oncoming Blazer. Should the car hit his, his body would snap apart under the force of impact. There was no way he would survive. But that was part of it – running a car so close you could taste death on your tongue.

How much time the Blazer had to react, how much room

it had to manoeuvre, Peter never knew. It could've been a
matter of not even a second, not even an inch. A hair's
breadth. The Blazer swerved past Peter's rear bumper,
nearly rolled, then sped out of sight. Peter came to a stop
and got out of his car. He felt strangely sober – a feeling
sharp and distinct. Like he'd come through to the other side
of something. He looked around for the girl. She had
disappeared amid the turmoil, a pale, luminous shade faded
into the dark.

There was no point in running. Peter placed his palms
against the side of the car and spread his feet. He waited for
the officer. He sensed his approach. He heard him say
something – 'You're in some deep shit, kid,' – and felt his
head slammed against the roof of the car, his arms pulled
back, twisted, and felt the cold clasp of handcuffs. He heard
the cop's hard instructions to get into the cruiser, and he felt
calm, without fear, like his life was out of his hands and this
was what he'd been waiting for, the deliverance he sought.

Something to Hide Away

I meet them at bars, usually – guys; though in the past I've let myself be picked up at the park in the burning glare of daylight, or at a bookstore or a café, and once even on the subway during the morning rush-hour when, amid the crush of commuters, a hand inadvertently brushed mine. Without knowing who the hand belonged to, I took hold of it. Our fingers intertwined. His thumb stroked my knuckles; his fingertips my palm. At the next stop, we let go. Of the people shuffling off the train it was impossible to tell who it might've been and for days afterwards I couldn't shake the bubbling, almost dizzying sensation the touch had caused.

Usually, though, I meet them in bars or clubs, in the half-light these places offer, during the confused, unaccountable hours between two a.m. and dawn, between the end of the day and the start of the next. A time when copulation becomes the only natural conclusion, a signifier to mark the passage of the day and the entrance to some other, secret world.

It's already well past the witching hour now and around me

in the small club there are no signs of it coming to a close. Dancers have climbed onto the bar. In the cleared space in the centre of the room others bounce and sway in time with the pumped-up reggae rhythm the DJ has going. The sweat of the crowd stains the air with a familiar odour that mixes with the cigarette smoke hanging from the ceiling and the occasional, pungent whiff of marijuana. On one of the couches in the far corner a couple are making out. From between the feet of two bar dancers I order a scotch, no rocks, and a shot of tequila. The tequila is for the guy I've been dancing with. Oliver, he says his name is. From Trinidad.

I saw him when he stepped into the bar with two other black guys some hours ago. His cousins. They own the Caribbean restaurant where he works as a line cook. He abandoned them almost immediately to talk to a stunning black girl on the dance floor. This was when my older sister, Janie, and her fiancé, Stephen, were still here. Over their shoulders I watched as Oliver worked his way through the room, a big smile taking his face every time he saw someone he knew. Eventually he approached me.

'I saw you when you came in,' I said. He held a cigarette between his fingers like it was a natural extension of them. He touched my spine.

'I saw you first,' he said. Then, as if I was someone he'd known all his life and had been waiting for me to arrive, he asked if I would dance with him.

Drinks in hand I return to the couch where Oliver is waiting. He lights a cigarette from the one he's smoking and places it between my lips, then instead of taking his shot runs his long fingers through my hair. His accent inflected by the sing-song of his native patois, he says, 'I love the fire in your hair.'

'Fire?'

'Yes. Fire.' It takes me a moment to realize he means the colour.

He says he loves the way the sun has made my freckles bleed into one across the bridge of my nose and chest and to illustrate this draws a finger from between my eyes down the centre of my face, over my lips and chin, down my neck. His finger comes to a stop at a point between my breasts where my tank-top won't let him go further.

'You are beautiful,' he says. I laugh, because I'm not – not glamorous or anything. Attractive, I think. Thin. And my face is one guys seem to like, innocent and protectable. I'm not beautiful though; not like Oliver. His face carved from obsidian, framed by a black burst of shoulder-length dreadlocks. 'You are intriguing,' he says. 'I want to get to know you.'

I came here with Janie. She and Stephen left while I was dancing with Oliver. Before they went she took hold of my arm. She said they had to work in the morning. 'You do too, Phoebe. You might consider coming home with us.'

'I'm all right.'

'Phoebe, be smart, you can't afford to fuck up any more.'

'I'm all right,' I snapped and turned away from her.

'Maybe we can leave,' I say.

Oliver shakes his head. His place is in Queens. I tell him I don't live far away.

On the way out Oliver touches my spine again and I take

his hand – a strange, sentimental act on my part. Outside, the street is slick and shiny from a rain shower that passed unnoticed while we were inside. It's still dark. In the east dawn threatens as a touch of grey crests the first low rooftops of the island.

'Let's run,' I say. 'I want to run.'

Oliver takes my hand. 'No. Let's not run.'

Before we reach the lighted intersection with East Houston I kiss Oliver, another sentimental act and something I can't quite explain. When I stop, Oliver holds my face between his palms. 'You have a beautiful face,' he says.

'Come on, let's run.'

I start away and do a handstand on the sidewalk, my short skirt slipping to my hips. My feet sway and drop. When I land upright, Oliver is in front of me. He kisses me, whispers that we should get to my place, no more games. Behind him all the way at the end of the island the Twin Towers rise from the nettle of skyscrapers. In the light they appear the same grey as the brightening sky. Except for the scattering of lighted windows that dot the length of the two spires, sky and concrete remain almost inseparable.

'I don't think I can wait that long. I might turn to stone with the sunrise. Or a pumpkin, or something ugly. You know us creatures of the night,' I cup my hand against Oliver's crotch. Through the leather of his pants I feel him grow hard – a sensation that always takes me by surprise even though it's hardly new to me.

Oliver takes my hand. 'We go to your place, OK.'

In the living room of the apartment I share with Janie I turn on Oliver. He tries to kiss me but I drop my head. I watch my fingers work his belt open. When he steps back, the two ends of his belt hanging open at his waist like an invitation, I ask, 'Why'd we stop?'

'You are a strange woman.'

'Don't call me that. I'm way too young to be a woman.'

'What is your age?' he asks, a slyness entering him. He is trying to know me.

'Twenty-two,' I say; a lie. I'm twenty-eight, going on twenty-nine. The thing is, I don't feel myself growing older. There's no evidence of the passage of time, of growth or change the way everyone says.

Oliver, I learn, will be eighteen in two weeks. I shake my head, both at how beautiful he is and at how young, though of course, like me, he could be lying. Could be lying about everything: his age; his job; his name. Why not? I did, told him my name was Camille. *Camille.* It's the name, as a kid, I'd always wished I'd had. *Camille.*

Oliver steps close. 'Does it matter, my age?' He smoothes a hand over and around first one then the other of my breasts, down my hip, my thigh, onto the bare skin of my leg.

'No,' I say and before he can do anything I kiss him. I pull him to the couch where he peels my clothes away. When he discovers it, he touches the gold hoop through my navel. He turns it in his fingers.

'It's one of my secrets,' I say.

He asks what my other secrets are and I slide his hand under my panties, over the smooth, shaved skin where my pubic hair should be. His finger dips easily into me. As he works at his pants I pull my panties off. I draw my knees to my chest. There are other secrets, secrets he'll never know.

Like all the guys who've come before him, who are inside me. Like the knowledge that I'm getting more out of this than he is; that this will make me powerful; that he is becoming a part of me, a part of my life, my being, another little something to hide away and keep for myself.

As he slides into me – another sensation both familiar and surprising – I close my eyes. I ignore his touching and lose myself to his presence. Not the motion, the slow, piston-like movement, but the fact of him. That he is inside me and will come there. That I can do this.

I tell Oliver to slow, to barely stir himself, and wrap my legs around his hips. 'I want to feel you,' I say.

Oliver presses his face into the crook of my neck. His breath comes in deep, even expulsions. He bites at my shoulder.

'Don't move,' I tell him. 'Just stay like this.'

'Make me disappear,' I tell him.

The first time I had sex I was nineteen, my sophomore year in college. It was with my boyfriend, Allen, the only real one I've had though there've been others I've been more or less close to. Whether or not I loved Allen doesn't make any difference now; he was a part of my life and for two years he remained one of the few boys I'd kissed and the only one I'd made love to. I didn't want anything else. As graduation approached, though, and the future loomed open and empty, I was taken by an urge to get away from all the constraints on my life, and while Allen and his buddies drank themselves blind at a Senior Week party I deliberately left with a guy I'd never met before and in an empty dorm room on a stripped mattress, the door open, whispered to him, 'I want you to fuck me.'

I never told Allen. I thought this one time would be it. A month later, though, having moved back in with my parents, I went home with another guy, then another. When Allen's father died I moved to New York to be with him. I stayed by him even as our relationship dissipated into weighted silences, until his need threatened to engulf me. When we broke up I asked him what his dreams were. He said he didn't have any.

It was after we broke up I started making up for lost time.

Above me now Oliver starts to move. He pushes deeper, harder, and I know I've lost him. He begins to grunt, little stifled cries like squeaks, and turns me onto my stomach. I watch over my shoulder. Then it's over and I'm aware of a touch of drool on my nape where Oliver pressed his lips when he came.

Day: I'm alone on the couch and it takes me a moment to figure out why I'm naked and hung over and not in my bed and why there's a naked black guy on the floor, his shirt pulled around his face and shoulders, his cock shrunken and wrinkled amid the tangle of tightly curled black hair between his legs. Then I remember.

In the kitchen I hear Janie and Stephen eating their breakfast. 'Well, if it's what she wants to do,' I hear Stephen say. 'I mean, it's her life, Janie, she can do with it what she wants.'

'Did you see them? Did you see? It's disgusting. They couldn't even make it to the bedroom.'

'What do you think? You think he has a—'

'Stephen! You're disgusting.'

Stephen laughs. One of them uses the steamer on the cappuccino machine. It crescendoes with a furious, frothy bubbling.

'If anything, he has a disease,' Janie says. 'You saw him, he looks like a fucking drug dealer. I mean, Jesus; AIDS, Stephen! This is New York after all. Not only is she ruining her life and about to lose her job – OK, whatever, if she doesn't care then I don't either – but this. She could die, Stephen. She may be dying now, she wouldn't even know.'

I don't know how many there've been; I don't count. One guy, though, one of the first while Allen and I were still together, I asked him how many girls he'd been with. Forty-three, he said. He was only my third and it made me want to catch up, which I'm sure I've since done. Of those I can think of six or seven I've tried to forget, encounters that leave me cold and alone with fear. One, we had sex right there in a club – a guy I remember only by the sharp sting of his cologne. We did it without speaking, no names; two strangers against a wall, half-real in the flashing strobe. It scares me. Sometimes I want to crawl inside myself, fold the world around me and disappear.

'Oliver,' I whisper. He doesn't stir and I try again.

From the kitchen Janie says, 'She's selfish, that's what she is.'

But what's the alternative? To be hemmed in by con-sequences and responsibility? To be restrained by faith? Possessed by love? It was see-you-later to those chains the first time I cheated on Allen.

Janie and Stephen clear the kitchen table, drop the dirty

dishes in the sink, wash, dry, put them away. I hear Janie walk into the living room, sense her behind the couch. She throws a small bundle against my chest. 'Put some fucking clothes on.'

Then she says, 'What the hell are you doing, Phoebe? What? What do you think—'

'Leave it,' I mutter. I use my clothes to cover my crotch.

'Leave it?' Janie, for a moment, appears flabbergasted. 'Jesus Christ, Phoebe, you bring a goddamn Rastafarian drug dealer in here and you want me to leave it? Jesus.' Stephen passes through the room, his eyes averted. He waits in the open doorway with his briefcase in one hand and Janie's in the other. 'I can't—' Janie flails her arms. 'You really don't care about anyone but yourself, do you? Do you? Can't you— Just look at yourself.'

'I said "Leave it," Janie.'

'No. No, I won't. I want him out of here.' She points at Oliver on the floor and I swear he twitches. 'Now. Now, Phoebe.'

'Yeah, whatever.'

She's about to say something else but Stephen tells her they're running late. She closes her eyes, takes a long breath. 'You're disgusting.' At the door she accepts her briefcase from Stephen, then slams the door shut.

Throughout this Oliver hasn't moved, probably faking slumber. I would. Kneeling beside him I move his shirt away from his face. Even in the light he's beautiful. Before I leave for work I throw a comforter over him and bring him a pillow.

Somehow I make it to the office on time. I work for an

advertising agency up on Lexington where Janie was an ad exec before getting a better position at another agency. She got me the job when I moved to New York, but four years later I'm still little more than a glorified secretary. I hate the job except for the short hours (I usually arrive half an hour late, take a long lunch and get out of there by four) and my boss's low expectations. Tina, my boss, has gone about as far as she will in the agency and lately has taken to worrying about me, giving me the inside scoop on promotions and offering to recommend me. She says I have a world of potential. The world is my oyster; she doesn't understand why I pass up opportunities at a good career. I don't have an answer she'd understand, a woman of her goals. I'm afraid of a future, afraid of its clear definitions and certainties, the shunting of possibility. So I tell Tina I'm waiting for my calling, that I'll know it when it comes.

At my desk I check my voice mail. Nada.

'Good night last night?' asks John, the guy who has the desk across from me. He notes my clothes, the same ones from last night, in an obvious way. 'Not really appropriate wear, is it? Management wouldn't be happy.'

'Fuck management.'

'So, let's hear it. Let's get the dirt.'

The usual: by lunch time I'll be the talk of this part of the office. Normally I contribute as much as anyone; I have no desire to lie about my actions or apologize. I don't pretend to be other than I am. But today I don't have any patience for the bullshit. The whispered words, the sudden silences when I step into a room. The looks and knowing smiles. 'No dirt,' I say. 'Nothing interesting. Nothing exciting.'

John gives me a sceptical look but doesn't say anything, for which I'm glad. I want to keep Oliver to myself.

As soon as I can get away, I head to the restroom. There, in one of the stalls, skirt hiked, I make myself come. It isn't difficult and I do it quickly and in silence, thinking about Oliver – though not the fucking or the feel of him inside me – or not just – but his face above mine in the half-light as he undressed me, almost invisible but for the impenetrable blackness of his skin; and his large, round eyes; and his hands, his slender fingers, white at the nails, creamy almond underneath; and the way he ran his fingers through my hair and touched my spine. As I begin to come, the restroom door opens and someone steps into the stall next to mine. I shut my eyes and let my mouth drop open. When I'm done, I flush.

Before I can get out of the restroom Tina steps from the other stall. 'Phoebe,' she says. Tina is a short, tiny woman in her fifties who has never married. A woman of great earnestness. 'Are you all right, Phoebe?'

'Yeah.'

'You're crying.'

'It's nothing. You know.' I wet my hands, wipe at my eyes and cheeks.

'I'm hearing things, Phoebe. Are you sure you're all right?'

'Well, I was on time, that's a start.'

'Don't joke about this, Phoebe. I'm being serious.' She takes my hand. 'If there's anything, please talk to me. You know it won't go past my office doors.'

Half joking I tell her I could use a raise, but Tina takes me seriously and says, 'You'll have to do better than you are.

You know I'll go the distance for you, but there's only so much I can do and certain people don't see things the way I do.'

I shrug. 'I know. But, you know, Tina, it's just a job. I just can't care that much about it.'

'Phoebe, some people don't have jobs. Fake it. How do you think I got to where I am? If the money is important to you, learn to fake it. Learn to care.'

'I just can't convince myself it's worth it.'

Back at my desk I check my voice mail again. A message from Janie saying she wants to talk to me. She wants me home tonight so we can discuss certain issues. There are no other messages.

I call home. I want to hear Oliver's voice, the rhythmic cadence of his accent. I want to know if he's comfortable and taken care of. Does he need anything? How could I have left him on the floor like that? Without even kissing him goodbye?

There's no answer and I wonder if Oliver is the kind of guy who'd pick up the phone in a stranger's place. Maybe he's still asleep. Maybe he's moved to my bed and wrapped himself in my covers. There's a thought I haven't had in a long time. Maybe when I come home he'll be waiting in my bed and will pull the covers aside and beckon for me to take my clothes off and join him, huddle beside him.

I call a second time. When the answering machine picks up I tell Oliver to answer. 'This is—' I pause, then say, 'Camille. From last night.' I imagine Oliver listening, smirking at my words, eating a bowl of cereal and drinking a cappuccino from the machine, watching cable or a movie or listening to CDs, smoking the last of my pot. If he looked through my dresser drawers he would've found my stash right on top next to my pipe and old letters and photos, most of them from college and of Allen.

Maybe he's not there any more. Maybe he left as soon as I was gone.

When I go to the smoking lounge for a cigarette it hits me: he could've cleared us out by now. It's past eleven, by now he could've sold the TV, the VCR, the stereo, our bikes, Janie's computer, her jewellery. The cappuccino machine even. He could've called his cousins the moment I left. They'd have emptied the place in half an hour; pulled a moving truck up to the door, thrown everything in back, told the neighbours we'd moved. That's the way it happens. No one says anything. Come home to an empty apartment with nothing but the answering machine sitting in the middle of the living room.

A cold stone of dread plunges into my stomach and I rush to my desk to call again. No answer.

In her office Tina is on the phone. She raises her finger for me to wait as I try to get her attention. *I need to go home*, I mouth. *Now.* I feel uneasy on my feet. All I want is to close my eyes in the hope I'll be transported away from here. I'm about to leave when Tina asks what I need.

'We've been broken into,' I sputter. 'I need to go home.'

'Oh my God. What happened? What did they take?'

I tell her I don't know. 'A neighbour called and said the door was open and everything was gone.' Tina gasps. My hands have become cold and I try not to wring them. 'I need to go,' I say.

'Have you called the police?'

'No, not yet. I want to go home first.'

'Do you want me to call?' Tina picks up the phone.

I shake my head, backing towards the door. 'No, no. I'll call.'

'What about your sister?'

'No, don't. No.'

I'm already through her door when I hear her ask, 'You sure?'

'Yeah,' I shout. John and the others in the office turn their heads as I rush to the elevator and when that doesn't arrive, to the emergency stairs.

Outside on Lexington I hail a cab. When we hit traffic around Union Square I throw the driver the fare, dropping my cigarette on the floor in the process, and walk. I try not to run. At Eighth Street I head over to Third Avenue, then Second. Across First, where I normally duck down to Seventh to avoid the crack house down the block, I spot a tall, black man with dreadlocks walking in the direction of the crack house. His shoulders sway when he walks, like I remember Oliver's doing, and he has the same confident, almost dream-like gait.

Even during the day black kids with guns tucked into their belts stand lookout on the corners here. They eye me as I pass. I don't look, pushing away the urge to run. Along the block two crack heads smelling of stale sweat, piss and vomit lie passed out on a doorstep, their heads nestled in yellowed newspaper. A third tries to hide herself in the bare shadow of a dumpster as she sucks on a glass pipe. Her eyes closed, she gives out a groan like in orgasm.

Ahead, the guy I've been following takes the steps of the

crack house. I catch his profile; it's not Oliver. His face is too fat. This does nothing to stem the anxiety growing inside me. How did I come to this? How could I have left Oliver alone in the apartment? This is it, the last one, never again. I'm becoming a fucking nun.

At the foot of the steps two strung-out hookers in tiny latex skirts and crimson brassieres and garish vinyl jackets stand ghostly in the light. 'Hey, bitch, you want some?' one hisses as I pass. The men sitting on the stoop, including the one I thought was Oliver, laugh. 'I bet you got a nice pussy. Come here, sugar, let me lick it.'

When I'm past I feel one anxiety lift, only to be replaced by another. From the corner of the next block I spy the stoop of our building. On the stoop a grey-haired black man, a retired vet, sits where he does every day. As I hurry by, he gives me a nod and says, 'Good day.'

Two flights up, the door to our apartment is closed. I put my ear against the wood. Nothing. No sound. I hesitate, then unlock the bolt. With my foot I swing the door inward.

Inside things are as I left them, except Oliver has disappeared. I check all the rooms. Everything is where it has always been. In the trash I find the note I left for Oliver with my work number on it, folded into quarters. I'd signed it, *Camille.* Except for this and my comforter folded neatly on the end of my bed there is no evidence of Oliver ever having been here. Not even a glass of water in the sink.

Gone, swift and traceless. Did it ever happen? Already the details seem vague.

Out on the steps I ask the man, the vet, if he saw Oliver leave. 'A black guy. Beautiful face. Dreadlocks.'

'Nope. Haven't seen a thing.'

'Are you sure?'

'The only beautiful face I seen come through these doors is yours.'

'Shit.'

Well, no burglary; sorry, Tina. I'm more than a little disappointed, really. Just another one of Phoebe's crises. This is a good one, though. Just went and completely flew the coop. No surprises there, right, Janie?

I return to the apartment and light a cigarette. The place has become hateful to me. The way it holds everything so neatly in its place: TV; stereo; VCR; bikes behind the door; CDs on the wall, movies on the shelves beneath them. And in the kitchen Janie's damn cappuccino machine snug between the microwave and the drying rack. The objects of settled life. The mundane. Everything I never wanted.

Because I need to do something with my disappointment, I take the cappuccino machine, go downstairs and set it next to the kerb.

'Broken?' the man on the steps asks.

'Yeah. Completely.'

The next time I come down with the VCR and a stack of movies. Then the rest of the movies and all the CDs. Then my bike, followed by Janie's. Next the microwave. And, why not, Janie's computer: printer, CD-ROM, monitor, everything, even the paper. Fuck it. I stack everything on the sidewalk.

'Could you help me?' I ask the man on the steps.

Together we bring down the TV. Then the couch.

'You moving or selling?' he asks. ''Cause if you're moving, I don't see no van and I wouldn't leave any of this stuff out on the street like that. Not with no one watching over it. Not around here, 'least. And if you're selling, well.'

'Neither. I'm just making space.'

The man grunts and shrugs. He is oblivious to the nervous relief I'm beginning to feel. I am committing an irrevocable act. I feel light, split in two, the one half of me doing and the other watching.

Once we have most of the big stuff down – the living room chairs, Janie's desk, the kitchen table – we start on the little things: lamps; framed posters from the walls; books and more books; my portable CD player; the blender; the vacuum cleaner; a fan. We set it all in a growing collection on the sidewalk where people have gathered to watch.

Two Ukrainian women whose neighbourhood this used to be have stopped on their way back from the grocery store. A couple of kids, black and white, too young for school, stand with their hands on their hips, while a homeless man picks at the items and looks around him but doesn't take anything. Three East Villagers with goatees and dirty dreadlocks and nose rings, smelling of incense, start browsing through the CDs and books. A little girl tries to get on my bike and falls.

'How much you want?' the guy looking at the CDs asks.

'She ain't selling,' the man helping me says. 'Not moving either.' He chuckles, shakes his head. This is the best thing he's seen in a long time.

'So, what's she doing?' someone asks.

No answer.

We do the beds next. First the mattresses and bedsprings, then the frames. We empty out the chests of drawers and bring them down. When a little girl reaches for my pot pipe one of the Ukrainian women smacks her hand and says something in her own language. A black boy follows us with a bundle of Janie's shoes in his arms. 'That's the idea,' I tell him, and we bring down all the clothes. We do the kitchen, then the bathrooms. Everything down to the shower curtain. The last things we throw from the windows. Socks, hats, scarves, more shoes, a pair of sandals, underwear, posters, an empty backpack, a wicker basket, a calendar. All that's left when we're through is the answering machine and telephone in the centre of the empty room, just the way I'd imagined it.

'Plenty of space now,' the man says.

I pick up the phone to call Janie. 'We've been robbed,' I tell her before she can say anything. 'They cleared us out. You should see the place; they took everything. It's like when we first moved in.' As if she can see through my eyes I look around at the empty space, at the light spots on the carpet where the furniture was, at the wall against which the TV once stood, where posters had hung. The room seems larger.

'Phoebe, what are you talking about? What's going on?'

'We've been robbed, Janie. Burgled. Broken into. Violated. All they left was the phone. It's amazing,' I say and begin to feel the lightness expanding from inside me.

'Jesus, Phoebe, are you all right? Have you called the cops?'

'They're on their way.' I start to laugh. At first it's a bubbling, then a burbling that soon grows into a fountain from down in my diaphragm up through my throat until it becomes a full-blown geyser.

'Phoebe, are you all right? You're not making sense.'

I can barely hear her.

'You should see the place,' I giggle. 'There's so much space. It's like new.' I hold the phone away and double up with laughter.

'Stay there,' I hear Janie's cry from far away. 'I'm coming home.'

And what will I tell her when she sees what's left of our belongings sitting on the sidewalk? Does it even matter? *Guess they just moved us out, Janie, changed their minds and left everything on the sidewalk, just like that. You know New York, it's a strange place. Shit happens.* What about the cops, what'll I tell them? *Sorry officers, but no one saw anything. I came home and this is the way it was, everything outside.* And Tina? *Well, Tina, there was this guy, Oliver, I met in a bar last night . . .* I step up to the window. Our stuff is still on the sidewalk, a big pile of junk. Most of the crowd lingers, hypnotized by our possessions, the only talking coming in hushed tones as if in wonder.

On the steps, in his usual place, sits the man who helped me. Like the others he takes in the product of our labour, not guarding it, just looking, watching the heap as if waiting for it to move, a slight glow of satisfaction on his face.

'I don't know what it is,' he says when I step outside, still laughing, 'but no one's taken anything.'

That's when I really start to lose it.

Part Two
WOUND AROUND THE TONGUE

Letters from Liam

Women are suckers for foreign accents, that's how I explain it.

I can still remember now, over a year later, when Lori first told me about Liam and what should've been their only, inconsequential encounter. She'd spent the summer backpacking around Europe and was due back in New York in two days. Calling long distance from Paris, her voice heady with excitement, she said that she'd met these two guys at the Oktoberfest in München a week before. 'One of them, he's Irish and a poet. He has this great brogue and tells these stories. It's unbelievable the places he's been and the things he's done. Run with the bulls in Pamplona; trucked through Africa; lived in Amsterdam. He's on his way to Australia by sailboat.'

It was exotic, I guess, and I should've known, but I was in love with Lori. Head over heels in love. I couldn't wait for her to get home so we could start our life together: the two of us stepping hand in hand through the future, over the hurdles set in our path, growing stronger and closer, falling deeper in love.

What a sucker!

Lori said she'd met Liam at the Hofbräuhaus. She was sitting with some Americans at one of the long tables in the beer hall when he'd stepped up. Said something like, 'Might a man of modest intent join this company of forlorn travellers.' According to Lori it was classic. I can only imagine.

All the hostels and hotels in the city were full, so after the Hofbräuhaus closed Liam led the entire crew back to the *Bahnhof* (Lori used that word *Bahnhof* instead of train station) where they slept on the concrete platform, news-papers pulled over them for warmth. 'It was everything my parents would hate,' she said. 'It was pure experience.' The next morning she and Liam smoked hand-rolled cigarettes in a café and in the afternoon went to the park and got high on hash.

'You hate pot,' I pointed out.

'Well, when in Rome. Besides, it was hash.'

They drank all night at the Oktoberfest and ended up dossing down (Lori's words again) in a VW minibus that belonged to a bunch of Australians they'd met. The next day they shared a train to Paris where a friend of Liam's, a painter, lived. It was from his flat Lori called. Liam, she said, had left for Valencia the day before.

'Why didn't you go along?' I asked.

'Are you jealous?'

'No.' I mean, I had a job, a future, and in two days Lori would be returning to all that.

Lori started in about Liam's poetry, how amazing and beautiful it was, all about the death of Irish gods and the sensuality, the raw lust, buried in Ireland's pagan past. His way with words, she said, was devastating. And he was nice, too. 'It's affirming to know there are people like that in the world, who are as kind and giving as he.'

And I thought I was one of those people!

Two days later Lori returned to New York. With a half-dozen roses I met her outside customs at JFK. Her hair was longer, straighter, its deep brown colour brushed with red highlights; her tan still strong but fading to her natural olive complexion. She looked thin. We kissed and she held onto me. In the taxi back to the city we didn't talk. At my place I drew a bath. I stared at Lori's chocolatey soft body submerged in the water. Later we made slow and careful love (I remember Lori naked, looking at me kneeling at the foot of the bed, spreading her knees, telling me she'd been waiting for this). Afterwards she fell asleep with her head on my chest, her hair still wet and fresh, and for a long time I stroked her skin and lost myself in her peaceful, sleeping face.

Lori and I had graduated from college together that May, me with a degree in Accounting, Lori as an Art History major. In June, while Lori went home to Whitewater, Wisconsin (a mere outcropping of buildings amid endless fields of corn), I moved into a three-bedroom apartment up on Eighty-First and Amsterdam along with two investment bankers I knew from business school. I started as an auditor at Coopers and Lybrand, my salary thirty-two grand plus overtime and bonuses. In three years, if I passed the exam, I'd be a CPA and could ditch Coopers; go private or to a smaller firm. Maybe something else altogether. Accounting was just a means to an end, a way of making money so Lori and I could get married, buy a house in Connecticut in a few years, start a family. The whole shebang.

As a graduation gift I bought Lori a ring. One carat. Not an engagement ring – not officially – but a ring no less, and you don't give one to a woman just like that.

Lori came to New York before she left for London. I took time off work (not necessarily a good move when you've only been there a month) and for three days we played like strangers in the city: did the Seaport and the Park, the Village; ate out for lunch and dinner every day, went to bars every night; got drunk off wine and vodka and laughed, laughed a lot. We made desperate, frantic, almost painful love in the alleys of the city, in restaurant restrooms and once in the back seat of a cab.

Our last night we rented a room at the Waldorf-Astoria and had dinner at the Four Seasons, which, along with everything else, seriously pressed the outer limits of my credit cards. Over dinner, two bottles of wine gone, I gave Lori the ring. She began to cry. Looking at it on her finger she said she was going to miss me and already couldn't wait to return. Back in the room she peeled my clothes away, pushed me to the bed. Kneeling naked across my body, she said, 'Don't do anything. This is for you.'

The next day on the way to the Grand Central we were quiet. Before Lori got on the bus to JFK, we kissed, then hugged.

'I want you to know I love you,' Lori said.

'I love you, too,' I said.

At home I rummaged through the stacks of photos from our two and a half years together. I was still awake when Lori called from Heathrow. In the background I could hear the sounds of the airport. She called again two days later, then not for another month and a half. In the meantime I got postcards scribbled with short, tight sentences about all the pubs in London and Edinburgh she'd been to; about a Scotch distillery in the Highlands; about the Louvre and the cafés and streets of Paris (her first time in Paris, before she met Liam); about coffee shops in Amsterdam and the city's red-light district with its live-sex shows and prostitutes waiting behind windows. The Museum of Sex. I got a card from Berlin where she went to all-night techno clubs in abandoned buildings in what used to be the Russian part of the city. She wrote about Prague's golden spires and cheap Pilsner and ecstatic Czechs in love with Americans. About drunken, sleepless train rides. Vienna, Venice, Geneva, Luzern.

I was happy for her, sure, but here I was working sixty, seventy hours a week at a job I hated except for the money, school loans and obscene credit card balances up the wazoo. At the same time I was scouting out jobs for Lori and looking for an apartment for her. So yeah, I was in a bit of a mood when she called after six weeks of silence to tell me about lying topless on gorgeous Spanish beaches and about Spanish men offering midnight rides on the backs of Ninjas or in their convertible 911 Carerras, proclaiming their immediate, undying love.

'I wish you could see me,' Lori said. 'I bought myself this tiny bikini. I'm tanned almost all over, even my boobs, and looking *hot*. My hair, I must say, is looking great. *I'm thin*.'

I made something up, told her I had to get off the phone. Ten minutes later she called back. She said she was sorry, she missed me and wished I was there. It wasn't as much fun without me.

'I want you to come back,' I said.

The postcards continued: San Sebastian, Madrid, Barcelona, Valencia, Marseilles, Florence, Rome. I didn't want to read them, but loneliness got the better of me. In September, a couple of days before she was supposed to return, Lori called again, this time from the Greek isle of Ios (where she was drinking ouzo and sunbathing nude on a beach full of gay men). She was staying in Europe an extra month. Her parents thought travelling was a good experience and would cover the costs.

'Have fun,' I muttered.

'Will you still be there for me?'

'I don't know.'

'I hope so.'

The next time she called was from Paris, which was when she told me about Liam. And maybe if she hadn't said what she did about hoping I'd be there when she came back, and if I hadn't been working such ridiculous hours, or if I'd had the opportunity to meet someone else, maybe I wouldn't have been waiting for her outside customs, a half-dozen red roses in my hand.

Lori lived at my place for two weeks before moving into a studio down in SoHo, between Prince and Spring. She said the Upper West Side was boring; she wanted to be where things were happening. She was ready to take the city by its balls and squeeze them until it cried, she said. She wouldn't be held back. A month later she landed a job as an Assistant

Account Executive at a small advertising agency in TriBeCa and began paying her own rent.

It must've been around this time Lori got the first of her letters from Liam. We were in some swanky SoHo bar full of the tall, tanned and beautiful of the glamorous downtown scene (among whom Lori fitted in well except for her glamourless hairstyle and the fact she'd gained back the weight she'd lost in Europe). We were good and gone from drinking eight-dollar Stolis when Lori asked if I remembered the Irish guy she'd told me about.

'No,' I lied.

'Liam. The Poet.' She lit a cigarette – a new habit – and tried unsuccessfully to blow the smoke away from us. She said he'd written from Australia and was flying to the States via Tahiti.

'Sailing didn't work out?' I asked.

Lori made an indignant expression. She said that when Liam got to LA he was going to buy a used car and drive up to San Francisco and from there across the country. He'd be in New York around New Year. 'I hope you don't mind, sweetie.'

In that same letter, as I know now, Liam (aside from going on about his travels) also wrote that he'd enjoyed Lori's *gracious and stimulating presence and awaited the day they might again share such delight.* Or something like that. 'Course, I didn't know that part, so I said, 'Just as long as we can be together for our anniversary.'

'Of course, sweetie.' Lori slid her hand down the inside of my thigh, dropping the ash from her cigarette on my trouser leg. She bit her lower lip in this way she had and smiled. 'Let's go home. There's something I want to do to you.'

*

Lori and I had met three years before at the New Year's Eve party of a mutual friend. I walked in on her making out with some guy in the bathroom. I smiled, said, 'Don't mind me,' then took a leak. Later Lori admitted she was glad I'd walked in, the guy had been a total sleaze. 'You're not a total sleaze, are you?' she asked. 'You don't look like a sleaze.' I told her I was the worst kind of sleaze – I was a sleaze who didn't look like a sleaze. Then I kissed her. She ended up kissing three other guys that night. When I found her passed out in the bathtub, I carried her to the spare bed and tucked her in. In the morning I woke with Lori snuggled against me on the floor where I'd crashed. We began kissing. She said, 'Don't think you're just another guy. None of the others got what I'm about to give to you.' Then she kneeled beside me, undid my pants and gave me the blowjob of a lifetime.

For our third anniversary I'd planned on a quiet dinner early in the evening before heading back to the party my roommates and I were throwing. As it turned out, though, Liam called the night before (having flown, not driven, from Vancouver). When Lori found out he was staying in some dive in Hell's Kitchen she invited him to stay with her. They went out. The next day, as arranged, I called about meeting for dinner, but she wasn't home and didn't get back until late in the afternoon.

'Are you pissed at me?' she asked. 'I'm a bitch. I'm sorry.' She and Liam had been out all night dancing. They'd had breakfast and gotten back only an hour ago. She dropped her voice. 'I'll make it up to you.'

She was late for dinner, of course, but the way she looked there was no way I could stay angry. She had on a tight black thing with a black choker snug around her throat and knee-high boots. 'Let's forget dinner,' I whispered as I led her from the taxi. 'Why don't we slip into the restroom or something, just as an appetizer?'

Lori gave me a wan smile. She fumbled for a smoke. 'I don't have the energy. I need a drink first, and some food.'

She grabbed the maitre d', ordered a Stoli, straight up, then made her way to the Ladies' Room. In my coat pocket I fingered the gold necklace I'd wanted to give her, but when she sat down, rubbing at her nose, trying to light another smoke, I changed my mind. I still have it somewhere, the necklace.

'Are you all right?' I asked.

'Just hung over; it's nothing.' Her eyes flitted from point to point about the room. I asked if she wanted to skip dinner.

'No, no.' She touched her fingers to my face. 'This is wonderful. I love you. I'll make it up to you, I promise.'

Dinner was a silent effort. Afterwards, as we walked without touching along Fifth Avenue, Lori said she wanted to take Liam to Times Square.

'Do what you want,' I said.

'Well, if that's the way you're going to be.'

'That's the way I'm going to be.'

I thought she would say something, but when I turned she was walking away with no hint of stopping. For a second there I thought of going after her. Instead I hailed a cab and went home.

By the time the party got going I was wasted and sat slumped on the couch in a shroud of drunken gloom. Sometime past midnight and the fall of the ball in Times

Square a girl sat next to me. I'd been gulping down all the abandoned glasses of champagne within my reach and I guess one of them was hers. Next thing, it's three in the morning and we're in a cab to her place in Murray Hill, her head resting on my shoulder, holding hands. On the sidewalk outside her building we mumble to each other, our faces close, lips brushing, then kiss. It took me a moment to stop. I pulled away from her, apologizing, and started walking. When I got home it was near dawn. Upstairs Lori lay in my bed, naked. I climbed in without undressing. Her eyes closed, Lori shifted, searched momentarily with her hands, peeled my pants open and pulled me on top of her. She wrapped her legs around my hips and gasped as I slid into her. I rolled her onto her hands and knees and started hammering at her. She turned to watch. Between deep grunts she moaned for me to push harder. As hard as I wanted. Just not to stop.

It was the first hate-fuck of my life. When I was finished Lori whispered, 'I told you I would make it up to you.'

Liam stayed with Lori for a week. I never met him and during that time didn't see Lori. I didn't want to talk to her. I'd thought of confronting her, but after that night I figured it best to let it go, that way get on with our lives. Lori, I figured, was thinking the same.

Some weeks after Liam left for Prague (the Paris of the Twenties, he called it) and around the time Lori got her second letter – in which he wrote that he'd *return as soon as fate will allow* – around this time Lori and I, one night after sex, lay in silence on her futon, the lights out, naked but not touching, pretty much the way it had been since New Year.

'This has been weird,' I said into the dark. 'What's going on?'

'It's because of Liam. You were jealous of him, weren't you?'

'Why should I be jealous? What's he got that I don't?'

'You want a list? For one thing, he's all man.' Lori paused, then said, 'Just kidding.'

'Well,' I said, 'I'm not jealous.'

'Bullshit. You were too.' Lori propped herself on one elbow to look at me. 'Don't tell me it didn't piss you off. Just admit it, Joe. It pissed you off.'

'It didn't.'

'You're so full of shit. If you were hanging out with some gorgeous French chick I'd tear your fucking balls off.'

'That's you,' I said.

'You're an asshole.' Lori turned away from me. I rolled close. I tried to put my arm around her, but she shrugged me off. 'Don't touch me, Joe.'

Liam was never mentioned again.

Over the next months I stayed where I was: Coopers and Lybrand; Eighty-First and Amsterdam; the only change, a raise and the fact my CPA had crawled another year closer. In that same time Lori – aside from having an active and vibrant correspondence with Liam, made *all the more alive and fragile for traversing the Atlantic and the half of Europe* – left the ad agency to work for a film director she'd met while shooting a commercial. News she apparently called Liam in Prague about before telling me. (By this time, figuring from Liam's responses, Lori had written that she hated her job at the agency, missed travelling and felt depressed, and that our relationship had become mundane and claustrophobic. In turn Liam wrote that she should leave me, *for it was obviously tearing at her soul to be caged by another's* – my! – *fantasies.*)

The director took Lori as her assistant on a feature film. Suddenly Lori found herself in a new world where she felt immediately at home. Whenever we talked now, which was every few days and usually on the phone late at night after she returned from the set, she always had something new to tell – which is probably why, even though we only saw each other one night a week, I began to believe things were improving and that our future together was again assured. This even as elements you couldn't call just friendly began to make their way into Liam's letters.

He began to include poems of his. I haven't gotten to read any of these, though, since Lori separated them from the letters and I didn't know to look. Without them and without Lori's letters to Liam, all I have to go on is what Liam wrote, which is more than enough. He was touched his poems had *so affected and moved* Lori, *even stirred something latent inside* her. When he composed a poem, when he *envisioned the beautiful sensuousness of being alive, an untamable passion gripped his soul as he wrought the words from nothingness and lay them down next to and atop each other, their energies brushing and becoming one.* Poetry? You could've fooled me. But what did I know? I was just a coat and tie. Just a first-year auditor for a giant, faceless accounting firm.

Because Lori and I barely saw each other any more I finally suggested we move in together. The problem was our separate leases. Mine came up in July; Lori's in November.

And the issue of where to live. Lori wanted to stay in SoHo, close to all the places she hung out now. The rents were ridiculous and I was thinking Gramercy or Murray Hill, but Lori refused to live north of Fourteenth Street and two weeks before I had to move out we still hadn't agreed on anything. What I couldn't know was that Liam had raised the stakes, betting a currency whose exoticism Lori couldn't resist.

He'd begun using the words *desire* and *passion* and said shit like the *enslaving infatuation of art*, going on about his attempts to *come to a better understanding of the ephemeral nature of living*, about how *wonderful and exciting it was to talk, even if only by means of this fragile correspondence* with someone of Lori's *sensitivity and breadth of understanding, who is so firmly in touch with her needs and wants and her emotions*. He wrote that he imagined Lori speaking the words she wrote to him – could *discern the echoes of her voice and the timbre of her accent* – that he needed to visualize her, so she would be real to him, or else, he felt, his words *would fall, forlorn, into the empty spaces between* them. He asked her to describe her room. What the light was like, how the air smelled. What sounds came from the street. Where she sat or lay as she wrote. What she looked at *when you lift your eyes from the paper, pen still in hand, and lose yourself to space and time.* It's enough to make you puke, but Lori, I guess, ate it up. She had her man across the pond weaving fantasies from thin air – fantasies no earthly person could ever give.

At the same time it was do or die on a one-bedroom walk-up in the part of SoHo that is almost the Lower East Side when Lori said she'd thought about it and didn't want to move out of her place. We'd just looked at the apartment and were eating dinner at an overpriced restaurant on West Broadway.

'So, should I get my own apartment then?' I asked. 'Do you not want to live together?'

'No, honey, no. It's just the lease.' She was thinking I could sublet a place until November, when her lease was up, then move in together. That way we could find something better, maybe closer to SoHo.

'That's hardly practical.'

From there it happened. Lori said everything had to run my way, nothing fit with what was easy for her. I reminded her that we'd already agreed.

'I don't remember agreeing to anything. You didn't leave me much choice.'

'Lori, we agreed.'

'Well, maybe I don't remember. Maybe I was drunk.' Lori lifted her glass to her lips. Her face blank and unquivering, she said, bam, 'This is indicative. It's over, Joe. Please just leave, I'll pay. And please don't call me and don't make a nuisance or an ass out of yourself. Take it like a man. You'll get over it.'

It's only now, having read Liam's letters, that I understand what happened.

After Lori called him in Prague about the film job, Liam wrote back that he'd *long been dissatisfied with the direction of poetry and the limited nature of the genre* – this despite having a private grant to support him in the pursuit of his art. He'd always hoped to branch out into film. He wrote that he'd love for Lori to help him get started in the business and would be back in New York as soon as possible.

Although fascinated by acting on the screen, it was his desire, of course, eventually to direct. Poetry, I guess, had worn thin on him.

In his last letter, dated two weeks before Lori brought the axe down on our life together, Liam wrote that he could wait no more. *My senses need to verify my imagination, for no beauty such as yours can be real. The anonymity of our correspondence that once inspired and moved me so now tortures me. I feel myself in a blackness. I need to see you. To touch your face and let my fingers swim through your hair and across your body, to be sure you are not merely an unearthly creation of my heart.*

The letter had him arriving at JFK two days after Lori's hatchet job and I can't help but wonder what happened between them that first night. Did they touch immediately and lose themselves in their longed-for kiss? Or were they cautious, nervous, coy even? Was it a game? How soon after they got back to Lori's cosy little SoHo studio did they make love? Did they wait until the latest hours of the night when all reason is gone, all conversation exhausted, giving in to each other finally as if they had no choice? Or did Lori drop her head into Liam's lap on the cab ride back and take him, Liam – Irishman, poet, traveller, fledgling actor – between her sweet, soft lips?

Whatever happened, I sure as hell wasn't on Lori's mind.

Things were pretty bad for me. In two weeks I'd be out of my apartment and so far had no place to live. My room-mates were useless: Bill was getting married and Mark came out of the closet and moved to Christopher Street in an effort to make up for ten years of repression and confusion. I hadn't told them Lori and I had split up, holding onto the hope it might all be a dream or, if it wasn't a dream, that a change in the alignment of the stars or a drop in barometric pressure might bring us back together again.

I lost it a couple of days before I had to move out. Until then I'd fought every urge to call Lori or walk to her apartment and stare up at her window, wait at the SoHo clubs where I was sure I could find her. Losing someone you love is like waking up to discover one of your limbs missing; it's not out of line to want to know why. So I called Lori at her apartment and left a message. I rang her beeper, without reply. I tried her apartment again. The fourth time I hung up. I thought about going over, breaking things. Or going to the film set, disrupting the shoot, confronting her with everyone watching, screw it.

My last legal night in my apartment (Bill and Mark had already cleared out and taken the furniture with them) Lori finally called. 'How are you doing?' she asked when I answered. 'What've you been up to?'

'Working,' I said. 'Packing. Cruising Forty-Second Street for sympathetic hookers inclined towards charity.'

'Are you holding up all right?'

'I'm fine. Just fine.' I was most of the way through a second bottle of red wine and felt sad and melancholy, which is what wine does to me. I told her I had a lot of questions.

'Well, there's some things you just can't know. You'll have to live with that, Joe.'

'Is there a chance? You know, for us?'

'My life has moved on, Joe. It's going directions I never imagined. There's someone else.'

♥

No surprise there, really. 'How cliché,' I said. 'Who is it? Not like I know him.'

'Liam.'

For a moment I didn't remember. Then I said, 'Oh, Liam. The poet. The one you were all hot and bothered about. He's back and he found you, how romantic.'

'Fuck you.'

'No, really, it is.'

'We had a correspondence,' Lori said. '*An active and vibrant correspondence.* When I saw him I realized I was in love with him. And he's in love with me. I didn't expect it and didn't want it, but it happened and I can't help that. We can't choose who we fall in love with.'

'Have you gone down on him?'

She grunted. 'What do you think?'

'I think everything in life is a choice. Who we love is a choice. There are no victims in love, only volunteers.'

Lori didn't seem to hear. 'I wish you the best,' she said and hung up.

I managed to get out of my apartment by the next afternoon, hung over to the point of puking, foggy about what had been said the night before. I had a feeling I didn't want to remember.

Because it was the only place I could think of that I could afford, I moved into the same hotel where Liam had stayed. Its tenants were mostly drug addicts – unreformed hippies; suburban runaways – hookers and drunks. Or else travellers and neo-Beatniks, looking for adventure, or the quintessential bohemian experience. I felt most comfortable with the drinkers, even though we barely talked and I was the only one with a full-time job. The drunks, I figured, had as little and as much control over the events in their lives as I did. Or thought I did.

My room was small and dank, in the back, with scant outside light. Its one window looked out on a brick wall across a narrow alley so close I could, if I reached my arms through the bars, touch it with my fingertips. At least it was a quiet room. I stayed through July, through the heat and humidity of August, when anyone who's able to leaves the city. In September, just as work got busy, I took a vacation to give myself time to find an apartment, maybe in my old neighbourhood or on the Upper East Side up in the Nineties where all the other young professionals straight out of college live. Instead I spent two weeks walking the length of the city from Wall Street to Harlem and back looking at nothing. Eventually I settled for a room in a converted hotel on Staten Island I saw advertised on my hotel's bulletin board. Right by the ferry port; its residents mostly semi-employed Vietnam vets on disability pay.

The day I was supposed to go back to work, I didn't. Called in sick, first one day, then the next, then didn't go at all. There wasn't any reason to now that I didn't have a goal to work towards, which is a strange, unsettling kind of freedom. It took getting used to. I was out of money and still in debt, so I got a job at a café in the Village. I didn't know anything about that kind of work, but had done time in the school cafeteria one semester my freshman year in college and what the hell. The pay sucks by comparison, the work is brainless but time passes and at least it's something. Keeps the days together.

A few weeks ago Lori called, having got my number from

my parents. I'd been hoping she would. I'd forgotten how deeply sexy her voice could be, though – how it could make my spine tingle and my face cold. She asked how I was, where I was living. I told her.

'What the hell are you doing on Staten Island?'

I said it wasn't a bad place; I had the ferry ride.

She dropped her voice that obvious notch deeper. 'Well, I have a new apartment. It's *totally* swank. One bedroom. Down by Broome and West Broadway. Really close to everything. You *have* to see it.'

I told her, yeah, sure. I would.

'I kicked Liam out. You know what they say: hot fires burn fast. He's apparently shacked up with some blonde bimbo with fake boobs out in Hollywood. He got this major part in a movie while working on our set.' Lori grunted with disgust, a sound frighteningly close to one she used to make when we made love.

'What about you?' I asked.

'Well, I'm dating this guy. He's in a band. He's English, has long hair.'

I didn't say a word. The next day I went to see her place. Liam's letters were on my mind, but I was curious to see Lori, too. She buzzed me in. She'd left her apartment door ajar and was in the bathroom, the door wide open so I could see her on the toilet when I came in. I asked if she wouldn't mind closing the door.

'Does it bother you? It shouldn't. Not after everything we've done together.'

She shut the door anyway.

In her bedroom I ignored the new photos propped on her dresser and went straight for the lower drawer of her bedstand where I knew she kept her personal bits. There, right up front, bundled together and tied with string, were a stack of letters. I checked for a *Love, Liam,* shoved them down the back of my pants and closed the drawer just as a flush came from the bathroom.

'There aren't any of Liam,' Lori said.

'What?'

She stood in the doorway, a glass of wine in her hand. It took me a moment to recognize her. Her hair was different, done up, styled. She was thin.

'I threw all his pictures out. Don't worry, I still have some of you. I didn't burn them.' She flattened her short black skirt against her thighs. '*So,* what do you think?'

'Nice.'

'*Very* swank, don't you think?'

I looked around. 'Yeah. The place is nice.' I scratched at the letters tucked under my belt to be sure they were still there.

'I meant me. I'm going to a record release party tonight at the Limelight.' Lori did a pirouette, her arms straight out. She wasn't wearing a bra and the black blazer she wore was cut to show the inside curves of her breasts, except they were too small for this and she too skinny and with her arms out she looked like a sunken-chested boy. She had a run up the back of her stocking. And I was curious how she could be so tan and so pale at the same time.

'You like?' she asked.

'You look nice.'

'Maybe we could have a drink.' She sat on the edge of her futon, her knees pulled up. From where I stood I could see the lace trim of her stockings around her upper thighs and the clasp of a garter and I wondered if she was wearing any underwear.

I told her I'd just come to see the place. 'It's nice. I'm glad things are working out for you.'

'It's about time.' Lori laughed, lit a cigarette. She'd gotten better at smoking. The ring I'd given her flashed on her finger. 'Come on, just one. It's *way* past my cocktail hour already. Besides, I miss you. I've been thinking about you.'

'I have to go,' I said.

Lori didn't stand to see me out, just watched from the bed, her face frozen in a half-smile, her cigarette in one hand, the glass of wine in the other.

Out on the street I had to contain myself. I didn't look at the letters until I got to the cheap bar on the Bowery I go to these days, around the corner from the Sally Army. I ordered a pitcher, poured a glass, drank it, poured another. Only then did I look at the letters. There were a lot of them, in no particular order. They looked like they'd been handled recently. I laid them out and rearranged them chronologically. As I read I thought about things I could do: tear them up, one by one; flush them down the toilet; burn them; send them to Liam out in Hollywood; make copies, marked with marginal notes, for all Lori's associates; maybe send them to her musician boyfriend from England. Anything to even the score.

The last letter in the stack was dated just a week before. *Dear Lori,* it read.

I am sorry to have left you the way I did. And I am sorry we could not have spoken, and for a last time let our eyes linger on one another, but, alas, words have run out between us. Hot fires rage only briefly before they die. I do not lie when I write that a part of me will always remember you.

It was signed, *With Love from LA, Liam.*

I rebound the letters. The next day I stuck a yellow post-it note to the top of the bundle. On it I'd scribbled, *Just needed to know.* I slipped the bundle into an envelope and mailed it, with no return address, to Lori. Some days later my phone rang, as I thought it would. I let it. It rang a couple more times over the next days, but I never answered. I figured it was Lori, and that is one person I don't ever want to see or talk to again. There comes a time events have gone too far and you can't ever go back and whatever it was you may have felt – love, hatred, sadness, spite – whatever it was, it's all gone. About the only thing I feel now is pity. Not pity for myself, but for Lori. Pity like I feel for someone who just doesn't get it, but even that wears off and eventually the phone did stop ringing.

Blame it on the Troubadours

My twin brother Jake, older than me by a minute and a half, and I share a beach house Jake bought a couple of years back when he sold the patent on a computer he built. Made a mint, the bastard, though he's never cared a whole lot about money. He's always been one of these indifferent geniuses, bored by the ease and simplicity with which everything comes to him. I remember when Rubic's Cube first came out, the first time he held one he finished it in under two minutes. He was ten. By the time he was thirteen our parents put him in a special school for the gifted, but through pure laziness he failed out in less than a semester and somehow ended up a year behind me back at the local high school. He caught up, and was offered early graduation. MIT, Rice, Chicago – they all came knocking. They thought he was going to be the next Richard Feynman. To the everlasting disappointment of our parents he turned them all down, stopped going to classes, spent his time on the beach playing arcade games day and night and getting stoned. When I finally graduated he went to the University of New Hampshire at the same time I did. Said if it was good enough for his brother it was good enough for him.

*

Eventually dropped out. Ended up building that computer in the basement of the house we rented near campus. The company he sold the patent to out in San Fran offered him a VP position, but he turned it down, bought this house and started freelancing. In the same time I've held about fifteen different jobs, never sure exactly what the hell I want.

Jake and I, we've had more than our share of fun in this house. We used to have parties here almost every weekend, returning after the bars closed to a fridge full of beer and a liquor cabinet stocked with all the necessities. I can't begin to count the number of times the two of us have sat on the back deck of the house watching the dawn come up over the ocean so drunk you think you've seen God.

Well, times change. You outgrow that, I guess. Jake's been seeing the same girl for over a year and now spends most his time at her place down in Boston. Heidi: tall, dark-haired and olive-skinned with big, round eyes, pouty lips and a body that could stun a steer at fifty paces. Another in a succession of beautiful women he always ends up with. A real firecracker. Me, I've been running a semi-voluntary dry streak, women-wise, for almost three years ever since things ended with my last girlfriend. These days if anything goes down at our place it feels more like a salon dedicated to the art of drinking. Me and Jake, Heidi, our old friend Bill and his new wife Anne. Occasionally one or two other people. We listen to music, smoke cigars, talk, drink. Along the way I've become a whisky man. Straight up. Jake is big on cocktails, and Anne and Bill are into vodka. Heidi, younger than us all by six or seven years and just out of college, likes to do shots and with her energy rules the salon. She has the knack, which is what it takes to drink properly. She's the one who gets us dancing on the tables and has us doing flaming shots of 151 and licking salt off each other's necks for tequila body slams. The others don't really like to keep up – especially Jake, who turns sour whenever Heidi gets partying – but I love it. Why wouldn't I?

Lately things have been bad between Jake and Heidi. Her father died a year ago and maybe that's taking its toll. I haven't seen Jake in ages; when he's not with Heidi he's been holed up in his room. He's on this medieval kick, I guess, reading all sorts of shit on the Arthurian legends for a video game he wants to design. So I told him I'd cook us all dinner. The five of us together. Get Heidi to have fun and Jake out of his room. Go all night. I've been taking a cooking course, paid for by Visa, with the vague idea of becoming a chef. Being unemployed I have a lot of vague ideas. I thought I'd try out a dish of swordfish over couscous and vegetables with a garlic tomato *beurre blanc*. Escargots in a puff pastry shell as an appetizer. To go with this, I buy a couple of bottles of Merlot and Anne and Bill show up with one of Chardonnay. Not quite the old times, but something better. Jake runs out to the packy and comes back with a gallon jug of Gallo.

He sees me make a disapproving face.

'Hey', he says, 'after three bottles it doesn't matter what the hell you're drinking. Wine's wine.'

He sets the bottle down, mixes himself a rum and coke and joins Bill and Anne out back while I handle the cooking. Soon Heidi, who spent the day at her mother's, is knocking on the door even though she has a key or could just walk around to the deck. She likes making an entrance, is all.

Likes to be let in. But Jake doesn't hear or is ignoring her and I have to abandon the food to get the door. She gives me a tight hug and a kiss on the mouth.

'Hi, sweetie,' she says. She touches the silk shirt I'm wearing. 'Nice. I like it.'

'Hey there, sugar pie.'

She holds up a bottle of something. 'Akvavit. It's Norwegian or Swedish. I want to make sure we all get loaded tonight.' She's tan, dressed in a short summer dress that clings to her body and leaves me confused about wanting to stare either down her cleavage or up her long legs.

Out on the deck she says to Jake, 'Like the outfit.' He's in his sloppies: ripped jeans; dirty, torn T-shirt. Heidi turns to Anne and Bill, both of them drinking vodka tonics with lime. 'I try to buy him something nice, you know, but he won't wear it. He's just not like his brother. No style. You could fool me they were twins.'

'I like what I like.' Jake shrugs. He takes a sip of his drink. 'This is who I am.'

'Jake, you're my brother and I respect and love you,' I say, 'but I have to agree: you have no taste. Except in women, of course.'

Heidi puts her arm around me and kisses my cheek. 'That's the only nice thing I've been told all day.' The sun is just starting to set behind us and reflections of crimson light catch on the abandoned strips of clouds that hang over the steel-coloured water. Heidi says, 'Hey, Jaker, I ran into one of your ex-girlfriends today. We talked about you.'

'Good for you.'

'Telling someone you talked about them with a friend is like the cruellest thing you can do,' Bill says. 'They immediately want to know what you talked about. It's like a power thing. I know something you don't know.'

'Not the Jaker, he doesn't care. Long's he's got a drink.' Heidi says it smiling and snatches Jake's cocktail from his hand and finishes it, but my guess is they've had another blow-out.

'That's right,' Jake says. 'That's exactly right. You got it.'

'And then there's talking about someone in the third person,' Bill says, but Anne has picked up on the little battle Heidi and Jake have going and touches Bill's arm.

'Well, if you made an effort at acting alive sometime,' Heidi says. 'What was it someone said: the opposite of love isn't hate; it's indifference?' Heidi mixes herself another drink from the liquor arrayed on the table. 'Anyway, your ex-girlfriend, Isabelle, she couldn't stop raving about you. What was it you did to her and why don't you do it to me, is what I want to know. Am I right or am I right, Anne? I mean, I want to know what I'm competing with. I just want to know where I stand. What I can expect. What number am I, right? Where do I fit in?'

'If this is what you need to be happy,' Jake says. He waves his hand at the air.

'There's a certain amount of accepting involved,' Anne, always diplomatic, says to Heidi.

Bill snorts. 'That's the truth.'

Heidi makes a face like everyone is against her, so I touch her hand and say, 'You're right on top, Heidi, of course, where you belong.'

'Tell that to your brother.' She finishes her drink. After a pause she laughs. 'See what I mean. You'd never think they were even related.'

*

In the kitchen I finish my dinner preparations. 'Let me guess, you guys had a fight,' I say to Jake, who's followed me into the kitchen.

'Yeah, what else is new?' The others are out on the deck. We can hear Heidi talking, saying how she loves to see Bill and Anne together, they're so cute, so perfect.

'So, what's up?' I ask.

'You know. Same old. She gets jealous. She needs attention. It's not just that she thinks the world revolves around her, she needs it to. I mean, I've been good to her. I mean, of course, with her father, you know, but there's a line. I'm not here to replace him.'

Heidi's father died of a sudden, massive heart attack. A year later she still hasn't gone to see his grave and even during the best of times she and Jake never talk about what happened.

'No, obviously not,' I say. 'You've already done more than most men, that's for sure. But that's you, isn't it?'

'You know what's funny. The sex is better than ever. You fight until your face explodes, then you can fuck all night like you're still angry. Like it's all you've got, you know. This afternoon, know what she said? She said she wants me to date other women. She said it's obvious that's what I want. She didn't want to break up and didn't want to date others guys, just wants me to be with other women.'

'Seems a little bit weird to me.' I finish my glass of Jameson's and pour another. 'Not exactly stable, if you know what I mean. Not exactly healthy.'

'Tell me about it.'

'Has she seen anyone? A shrink? Maybe it would help.'

'She went once and didn't go back. She's afraid of disaster, is the thing. She's afraid of any little thing going wrong instead of going the way she hoped.'

'Maybe this isn't the right thing to say, but maybe you should leave her, Jake.'

Jake takes a sip from his drink. 'It's not that easy.'

Jake and I bring the appetizers out onto the deck. I see Heidi turn her eyes on him. We put on some music, pass the wine. All the while Jake and Heidi sit across from each other, not speaking to each other. By the time we get to the entrées the sun has set and the only evidence of the ocean nearby comes from the crash of waves giving their rhythm to the night.

'This is just amazing, Wayne,' Anne says in reference to the food. 'Wow.'

'He cooks like this all the time. Like it's nothing,' Jake says. He reaches for the Gallo, pours himself a glass, then hands the bottle on.

'This is the kind of crap gives you a headache while you're drinking it, then burns when you piss,' I say. 'Where the hell do you get this shit?'

'Hey, it's cheap and there's a lot of it.'

'Cheap and lots of it, that's the Jaker for you,' Heidi says. 'That's my hunk o' love.' Heidi loops her arm through mine, accepting the bottle with her free hand.

'It's not like you don't make money, Jake,' Bill says and Anne gives him a look.

'No, it's not,' Heidi says. My guess is she was drinking before she showed. Jake was. I was.

'Are you still doing that job for Citibank?' Bill asks.

'No,' Heidi answers before Jake can. 'They wanted him to start up a new system for their direct deposit, but he turned them down. They offered to practically double his salary, but he still said no. Can you believe that? What kind of person does that?'

Jake shrugs. 'I don't deserve it; I'm not worth that much. It seems ridiculous to me to pay like that for something any asshole can learn. It's incongruous. I mean, I don't do shit. I'm hired for a thirty-five-hour week and am usually out by four, three-thirty. It's a fucking joke.'

'So what do you want to do?' Anne asks. 'What would challenge you?' She's a school teacher and has a school teacher's sensibilities.

'I don't know. I'm thinking about designing a video game. At least it's something to make someone's life a little happier, I mean, if that's what they're into.'

'Honey, you have talent,' Heidi says. 'Don't you think you're wasting it? You could do anything.'

'What's the big deal about talent? It's overrated. People just want to take it from you and use it for their own ends. That, or they're envious because it makes them feel small. Talent is a commodity. It's just another expectation. Something people want from you. I'd rather just do what I feel like doing and fuck 'em. I'm happiest when the world can't touch me.'

'Some of us don't have that luxury.'

'I'm more than aware of that.'

'Some of us don't have a choice.'

'So what do you want from me? Tell me and it's yours.'

'I want you to do what you feel like doing, honey.'

Jake reaches for the jug of wine. He empties it into his glass. 'Well, right now I feel like drinking. I feel like enjoying dinner with my friends. I don't want to think about anything. Is that too much?'

'Here's to all of us,' I toast.

'Nothing is ever so bad,' Bill says. 'You'll learn that, Heidi.'

'Or so good,' Anne adds. 'That's what it means to grow up. Things just happen.' But Heidi doesn't look like she believes either of them.

We raise our glasses. Heidi glances at Jake as he finishes his wine, then at me.

When we're through with dessert and back into the liquor, Heidi announces, 'Jake doesn't love me.'

Bill and I smoke our cigars. Across the ocean the moon has long ago come up and its light sparkles on the water. Jake stares out at the ocean as if he's trying to find something there he can't find anywhere else. 'I blame it on the troubadours,' he says out of the blue without taking his eyes from the water. 'They're the ones who invented love as we know it. A total fucking fabrication. They invented all of it, the legend of Lancelot and Guinevere. A romantic creation.'

'Whatever that means,' Bill laughs. He tosses a bunched up napkin at Jake's head.

'What the hell did they know about love?' Jake says.

'Of course he loves you,' Anne says. She's moved her chair closer to Bill's. They hold hands, and now and then Bill lifts hers to his lips and kisses her fingers. It's something as simple as that can cause a pang in my heart.

'No, he doesn't. If he did he wouldn't be scared to touch me.'

'How could anyone be scared of that?' I say.

'He'd rather stay up until dawn drinking. Or playing video games.'

'The dawn's overrated,' Anne says. 'A friend of mine and I, when we were in college, we once stayed up all night doing Ecstasy. We went to the beach to skinny-dip at sunrise. We had some kind of bucolic catharsis in mind, I guess. Well, the water was freezing, you couldn't see the sun because of the cloud cover, we were hung over and the bugs were crazy, eating us alive. So much for that.'

'It's like sex on the beach,' Bill says. 'Looks romantic, but all that sand getting everywhere is a pain in the ass; so to speak.'

'That's what I'm saying,' Jake says.

'You would know, too, wouldn't you,' Anne teases Bill, ignoring Jake.

'Look at you,' Bill says. 'School teacher, taking Ex all night. Who was that with? Gary? Chuck?'

'Get over it.'

Heidi presses her shoulder against mine. Her hand falls on my thigh. Quietly she says, 'You wouldn't be scared, would you? I'm good-looking, I'm attractive. You'd kiss me, wouldn't you?'

'Of course I would.' I kiss her on the cheek.

'You're sweet to lie to me.' To Jake she says, 'See, Jake, your brother thinks I'm beautiful. I bet he thinks I'm the most beautiful woman in the world.'

'Hey, if that's what you want to hear.'

At the other end of the table Bill kisses Anne on the nape

of her neck. She closes her eyes and tilts her head just a touch, exposing more for him to kiss.

'Maybe I should take him home,' Heidi says.

'It's a free world,' Jake says. 'I'm not stopping you.'

'I don't understand you. Why are you like this?' Heidi's voice has turned brittle, threatening to grow loud. 'No one in the world is like this.'

'No one in the world is like anything.' Jake keeps his own voice even. 'I don't really go around comparing. It only leaves you disappointed.'

'Maybe you should.'

'How about some akvavit?' I shout and stand.

I'm in the kitchen only a moment before Jake comes in.

'So. Tension.' He speaks slowly. A slight grimace of pain twists his mouth.

'Jake, listen, this is your business, but you're going to have to do something. That's what it comes down to. I mean, she's coming on to me.'

Jake mixes himself a Captain and coke. I wait, but he doesn't say anything.

'So?' I ask.

'So, go ahead. If you want. It's a free world.' He picks up a wrapped cigar, twirls it in his fingers, then puts it down. 'How the hell can you guys smoke these things? Don't they make your mouth taste disgusting?'

'Jesus, Jake. You're not doing anyone any favours. It may be she doesn't see things the way you do. You can't expect her to.'

Jake pours each of us a shot of akvavit to go along with the drinks we already have. 'You know, Wayne, it's not all it appears. It's not about need, but about taking. I want, I want, I want. Give me, give me, give me. Make me happy. I'm fucking sick of it. Everyone wants a part of you. They need to bring you down to their level. It's a fucking power struggle, like she's fighting to gain control of me, I'm not into it.'

'Well, then leave her. Or talk to her.'

Jake sniffs his drink, swirls it around the glass, finally takes a sip. 'Except, the thing is . . . There are moments, you know, when none of that shit is there, none of the selfishness, moments that, you know, they could go on forever and you're not thinking about anything else. Like it's not even you any more. That kind of thing. It's hard to remember anything else. Is that love? Because it ain't what I used to think it was.'

He lifts his shot of akvavit and I follow suit. It tastes like rye-flavoured vodka. Before I can say anything else Heidi comes in. 'Why don't you keep Anne and Bill entertained while I talk to your brother, Jakey. I think they're getting a bit frisky.'

'Maybe it's you two—' I start.

'No, no,' Jake says. He leaves without even a look at Heidi.

Heidi lifts herself onto the countertop beside me. She takes the bottle of akvavit from between my legs and tilts the bottle into her mouth. As she lowers it the shoulder strap on her dress slips down her arm. 'So, what were you two saying about me?'

'Nothing. We weren't talking about you.'

'And I thought you two shared everything.' She takes the cigar from between my fingers and puffs on it. 'I thought I'd be the most immediate and engaging topic of conversation among the Gallagher brothers. The fabled Gallagher brothers. So tell me, have you two ever slept with the same woman?'

'Not intentionally.'

'How about at the same time?'

'That's more than I want to see of my brother.'

Heidi does another shot. 'I can't figure him out. You know it's been over a year and he still hasn't said he loves me.'

I take the bottle from her. 'I went out with a girl for three years. I told her I loved her the first time I saw her, before I even knew her name or kissed her. You know what happened? We ended up beating each other up. I mean it. We started fighting and she'd start hitting me, in the arm like, going at me—'

'Maybe that's what Jake needs.'

'She got me going once; I threw a glass, smashed the thing against the wall right next to her head. She threw a lamp. I'm not a violent person; I've never hit anyone. But love will fuck you up.'

Heidi looked at me. 'I'm sorry, Wayne, I didn't— But at least it's something. At least you two felt something. Passion. With Jake who the fuck knows?' Heidi puts her head on my shoulder. Her hair touches my face. It smells of apricot and is soft on my cheek. I want to lose my hands in it, want to lift it away, kiss her nape, brush the other strap off her shoulder, bury my head in her breasts.

'Know how it ended?' I say. 'She was having an affair. There we were, tearing each other's heads off and the whole time she's fucking someone else. That's the kicker. Thinking that instead of me, it could've been this guy she was throwing lamps at.'

'But you loved her?'

'Yeah, but by that time all I wanted was peace.'

'You don't think I'm like her, do you? I'm not. I just need to know that Jake loves me. You do think he loves me, don't you, Wayne?'

But I can't answer that. Who am I to know what's in my brother's heart?

'Do you think if you loved me it would be the same?' Heidi asks. 'I bet people wouldn't even know it was you. They'd think you were Jake. I bet in bed I wouldn't even know who was who.'

'I think you're drunk, Heidi.'

She brushes her fingertips across the top of my hand, then takes my hand in hers. 'You know today is the first anniversary of my father's death. I should be mourning. But here I am, drunk with my boyfriend's twin brother. And where's my boyfriend?'

'Why don't we go outside and dance?' I move away and pull her down from the counter. 'Let's have ourselves a good old time of it, get the Jaker going.'

She lifts her head. 'Why can't you be Jake, Wayne?'

Out on the deck Anne is sitting in Bill's lap. Both their hands are intertwined. Jake is talking.

'Let's have some fun,' Heidi shouts. She turns off the music and puts in a new CD. 'Let's dance.' She raises her arms above her head, does a sexy turn, swaying her hips. In her armpit I can see where she cut herself shaving, just a small, thin line of hardened blood.

Bill makes a show of looking at his watch. 'We should go. It's almost three.' In unison he and Anne get up. I walk them to the door. He says, 'We have to go to church in the morning. Anne's parents are in town.'

'Bill! Don't give him that. We go to church every Sunday.'

'She makes me.' Bill has his arm around Anne.

'No, I don't. You're the one who wanted to come along.' Anne is smiling, her cheeks rosy from drink. She holds onto Bill's hand on her waist, leaning into his embrace. 'It's just you'll feel guilty after what I'm going to do to you when we get home. You'll want to spend a whole week in confession.'

'Confession, Bill?' I raise a brow. 'I can't see you in confession. Where the hell would you start?'

'I went Catholic when I married Anne.'

' "Went Catholic." Listen to him,' Anne says.

'Maybe I should go along to corroborate, make sure you're giving the priest the whole truth.'

'Oh, Jesus, that's the last thing they want to hear. They're like women that way.'

'Bill.' Anne gives him a stab with her elbow.

I watch them walk down the path to their car. Bill gets in first, then opens the door for Anne. He turns on the engine but not the lights. They wait a moment, honk the horn, then drive away, their lights still off. Neither of them mentioned Jake and Heidi, though I'm sure they're talking about them now on their drive home. Talking about how glad they are to have each other, how lucky. Eventually the conversation will die. Maybe Anne will lean over from the passenger seat, kiss Bill on the ear, the jaw, the side of his neck. She might put her hand in his lap. Maybe he'll pull over, or maybe continue driving. At home they might make love or pass out. In the morning they'll go to church.

When I return out back, all hell has broken loose. An old Eric Clapton song is playing: 'Wonderful Tonight'. According to Heidi it's her and Jake's song. It was playing on the jukebox the first time they kissed. This happened before her father died. I remember, Jake came home from a night out boozing and kept me up the rest of the night. He couldn't stop going on about how wonderful and beautiful this girl was he met. She was visiting from Boston. He couldn't stop talking about her. He'd do anything for her, he said. If she required him to drag his balls across a mile of broken glass, he would do it, and smile all the way. For two months I barely saw him, he was always heading down to Boston, taking her places, out. Buying her flowers. He said he felt ten years younger, except happier. Then her father died and everything changed.

Now Heidi is screaming at Jake: 'What the hell is wrong with you? I don't get you. What's wrong with you?' She has the bottle of akvavit in her hand and I'm afraid that at any moment she's going to smash it over Jake's head. Jake doesn't seem to notice, or care. He sits in his chair looking at the space where Heidi happens to be standing. You might think he was stoned. Like he's gone numb.

When she sees me, Heidi points, 'Your brother here won't dance with me. You'll dance with me, won't you?'

I try to get the bottle from her, but she holds onto it and takes another hit. I look over at Jake. Heidi doesn't notice, and even if she did she probably wouldn't recognize it, but Jake gives me a look like he's begging me not to dance with her. A look maybe only a brother can know.

'See, Jake, your brother will dance with me.'

Heidi folds her hands behind my neck and brings her hips against mine. Her breasts brush my chest. I put my hands on her waist. She is warm, almost hot, and soft. I imagine pressing my cheek against her stomach, imagine kissing her navel, feeling the tickle of her pubic hair against my lips. I want to fold her around me.

'At least somebody loves me,' Heidi says. She buries her head against my shoulder. I look at Jake, but can't get myself to meet his eyes, afraid it will be like seeing into a mirror, so I find a spot just beneath them on the bridge of his nose where I hope he won't notice I'm avoiding looking at him.

'Go for it.' Jake says. 'Nothing like a new sensation. It's a free world.' Jake takes a sip of his cocktail, then another. When he finishes he walks to the kitchen. Over Heidi's shoulder I empty what's left of the akvavit into my mouth. I'm drunk and am having trouble standing. I have to hold onto Heidi.

'Go talk to him,' I say.

Heidi lifts her head. Her cheek brushes mine. 'It's too late for that. There's nothing to talk about. I love him; he doesn't love me: what's to talk about? He doesn't care what I do. He doesn't care about anything, not even himself. I just don't understand it. He has so much going for him. He could do anything.'

'He's strange that way, but he's a good person.'

We turn slow circles, barely even dancing.

'I know,' she says. 'That's why I fell in love with him. He was so good to me after my father died. He's been so good. A lot of guys would've left. But he stayed. He wouldn't have it any other way, you know. There wasn't even an option for him. When I asked him, he said he'd never even considered anything else.'

I nod. 'When we were kids,' I say, 'he was always being put in special classes for the gifted, you know, but he'd always cry and refused to do any work until they put him back in my class. He was eight years old and there he was saying he wasn't better than anyone else. He was just like anybody.'

'But he's not. Doesn't he understand that?' Heidi grips the back of my head. She runs her fingers through my hair.

'He used to help me with my homework,' I say. 'He wouldn't give me the answers, but would ask me questions forcing me to think until I got the answers myself. That kind of thing. In college for a while, when I was toying with religion, he did the same thing, just kept on asking me questions about what I believed. He wanted me to think for myself and figure it out for myself.'

Heidi lifts her chin from my shoulder. 'But you do think there's a God, don't you?'

'I'd like to, but I don't know if I can.'

'Jake doesn't. He says we're here on our own. There has to be, though. I can't think my father isn't someplace waiting for me.'

'You know what he did once?' I spread one hand over Heidi's hip and feel its soft, warm jab against my palm. I pull on the thin fabric of her dress. 'I was having a fight with my mother and she slapped me. This was in high school. We must've been fourteen or fifteen. My face was all red and stung and I was crying. Jake said you could still see the hand mark. He told our mom that she would never do that again. Never. That's what he said. She was already feeling guilty and this just nailed her, like she'd struck the both of us at once. Her prize boy and the fuck-up. But she didn't understand the way we were connected.' I try to take another hit off the bottle but the bottle's empty. The song has ended, gone on to something else, but we continue our circles, shuffling, holding onto each other.

'What happened to him, Wayne? What? Why doesn't he love me?'

'Maybe he does.'

Without warning Heidi kisses me. It's not what I expected, but I don't stop her; I kiss her back. Her lips are soft. She withdraws slightly to look at me. Maybe she's trying to figure out who I am: Wayne or Jake. Does it matter? Afraid of what she might see, I kiss her again. She responds, then stops. I slide my hands from her waist to the bare skin of her thighs, under the skirt of her dress, up until they met the curve of her ass. My palms, my fingers feel on fire.

'No,' Heidi whispers.

I kiss her again. Kiss her neck, her ear. She does nothing to stop me. Just hangs in my arms. At any moment I expect to see Jake standing in the living room watching us through the screen doors, and I wonder what I would do, but he doesn't appear. When I try to find Heidi's lips again she's crying. I want to hold her to me, but she disengages herself and walks through the living room to the bathroom. She shuts the door behind her, not bothering with the light.

In the kitchen I find Jake sitting on the counter drinking another cocktail, examining an unlit cigar. He holds it between his fingers as if he were smoking it.

'I like holding them,' he says. 'It gives you something to do with your hands. It's satisfying.'

I pour myself a shot of Jameson's and sit down across from him. He doesn't look at me. He twirls the cigar in his fingers, watching it go round and round. I try to say something.

'Is there something wrong with Heidi?' I ask.

'What do you mean?' Jake looks up. 'You mean unusually wrong?' He shakes his head. 'I'm not sure what else I can do, Wayne. I can't leave her, not in her state. I love her, but there's nothing left inside of me. I'm running on fumes.'

I'm not really listening. His words are only sounds.

'Maybe someone else . . . I don't know.' He chuckles. 'Maybe this is how King Arthur felt.'

'Yeah, maybe,' I mumble, unsure what he's talking about, if he knows what just happened between me and Heidi, if that's what he's getting at. I don't say anything else.

Jake puts the cigar on the counter and slides off. 'Heidi in the bathroom?' he asks. I nod. 'I should go get her,' he says.

He makes his way to the bathroom. I hear him knock quietly on the door. I hear him whisper Heidi's name, open the door, close it behind him. See the light go on. I look around. I pour myself another drink and with glass and bottle go out back. Alone, I take the steps down the side of the deck to the rocks below where the waves suck and seep in and out of the empty pockets between the rocks. I'm too drunk already for it to matter any more if I keep going – dawn or not. For a moment there I think I can already see it coming, but it's only the lights off the highway; sunrise is still a long way away. With any luck I won't remember any of this in the morning. If you don't remember it, it never happened. It's something you tell yourself.

Don't Speak to Me of Love

Ben and Allison fell in love when Ben was in his last year of college in Boston. Allison was a freshman, just eighteen; they met during her orientation week. He was the first boy she ever made love to. Afterwards she told Ben she knew as soon as she saw him on her first day that he would be the one.

'I've been in love, but never like this,' she whispered.

'I've never been happier,' Ben whispered back. 'It's like I've died.' He'd never been in love. Hadn't thought it possible. For both of them, in their different ways, this was a first.

Whenever they fought, afterwards, in the tender warmth of reconciliation, they told each other, 'We're still learning. This thing we have, it takes work. We'll make it through.' It made them feel older to believe this. More mature, like they were coming to grips with life and all the surprises it had to offer: the two of them together, battered warriors – scarred but smarter. That was how Ben described them.

In the spring of his senior year Ben discovered that he'd missed the deadlines for application to graduate school. His intention, for lack of any other, had always been to become an English professor. Language came easy to him. He felt comfortable in the closed, secure environment of a university. Of all the writers he'd read, Joyce had moved him the most. *A Portrait of the Artist as a Young Man* still made his spine ache. He imagined himself teaching Joyce, Yeats, Eliot. Imagined himself as a passionate, inspiring professor. The rapt attention in the eyes of his students as he spoke.

'You can apply again next year,' Allison said when he told her how he'd called several universities that day without any luck. He was too late. 'Come spend the summer with me in New York. We can get a place together. You can work there.'

Ben didn't say anything. For all that he loved Allison and found himself drawn back to her touch whenever he thought about leaving her, he had an idealized notion of facing the future on his own terms, alone, and he'd convinced himself the future would begin sometime following the summer of his graduation, in September; about the same time the next semester started.

While Allison talked up plans for their summer in Manhattan, Ben went to one of his professors, an émigré from Ireland who had taught at University College Dublin. He told Ben he'd talk to his colleagues in Ireland, see what he could do. Things worked differently there, he said. When Ben told Allison the news her features drew themselves into a sullen mask, imperceptibly alive. For an hour she refused to speak. Finally she asked, 'And what about us?' Ben had no answer. He'd never thought beyond this point. He didn't trust his emotions – they were too fickle, and just the thought of Allison wreaked havoc on them.

'This isn't what I thought love would be like,' he said.

'This is it, Ben,' Allison said. 'This is love. This is as good as it's going to get.'

After his graduation Ben moved back in with his parents. He helped his mother in the garden, his father paint the house; read a lot; went to the beach; drank – every Monday, karaoke night at Banana's; Thursdays on the porch at Poco's; late night at the Excalibur. By July he still hadn't heard any news from his professor about Ireland. Allison had returned to her mother's on Long Island for the summer and in the first weeks she and Ben spent drawn-out hours on the phone consumed by silence. 'This is ridiculous. I'm coming down,' Ben finally said.

That afternoon Ben drove to New York. With the money he had he rented a hotel room on Sixth Avenue near the park. He and Allison went for long walks in the city and talked. At night, in the dark, they made love. They took their time, never wanting it to end. 'Let's just enjoy ourselves,' they said. 'Let's live while we can in the time we have and not think about the future or what will happen. We can't know that. We can't ever know what will happen.'

'Never say never,' Ben said.

'Never say never.'

Their belief in those words kept their feelings alive over the distance that summer and every other night they talked on the phone. Suddenly there was so much between them and so much to share in the little time they might have left. They held nothing back. Allison would lie curled in her bed in the dark and listen to Ben tell her in hushed tones how he missed her voice, its low, sulky timbre, and craved the comfort of her presence, her warmth folded against him. The whispered touch of her dusky skin on his, the wash of her black hair like water on his face as she bent to kiss him. He wanted to crawl inside her.

'I wish I could make love to you,' Ben said. He described what he would do to her, where he would touch her, kiss her – the trace of his fingers on her body, the legacy of his lips on the inside of her wrist, the hollow of her arm, the crook of her neck. He described his eyes lingering on her. Described himself inside her. How she would feel. When all words were lost they listened for minutes to each other's breathing, as if that way to escape their bodies.

As fall approached and Allison had to return to school, she talked about the two of them moving into an apartment together in Boston. 'Wouldn't it be fun?' She began scouring the papers for apartments. The day before Allison's nineteenth birthday, Ben heard from his professor. His application had gone through, he'd been accepted into the doctoral programme in English Literature at University College Dublin. The semester was to start in one month.

At Logan airport on the day of Ben's departure he and Allison sat in the bar in the international terminal. They watched the airport in noiseless motion beyond the thick windows: the great albatrosses approaching from out of the firmament and lowering through the sky until stopped and still on the ground while buggies zoomed and zipped without pattern across the tarmac to attend to the mighty creatures, the people on the tarmac dwarfed by the workings surrounding them as behind, other planes lumbered aloft and free from the pull of the earth. In the booth Ben clutched Allison to him. He said everything would work out for the best. They would be all right.

'I know,' Allison said. She had begun to cry.

'Life is moving us on,' Ben said. 'We're young still.'

'I guess it's what you have to do. It's just, I never wanted to believe it would actually happen. I thought we'd spend the rest of our lives together. I can't imagine living without you.'

Ben became maudlin. He thought about what he knew would happen given distance and time, if not immediately, then when the phone calls became fewer, their letters thinly coated with conviction – hurried, offering only the barest facts about their lives moving inexplicably apart. 'Friends for life,' he promised. It didn't seem impossible.

He went to kiss Allison, but she stopped him.

'No, Ben,' she said. 'We can't.' She offered her hand instead.

A month later Ben sat in McDaid's pub on Harry Street in Dublin drinking a pint of Guinness and talking with an old man who claimed to have known Yeats, when his flatmate, Nick, found him. Nick said there had been several messages from Allison on their answering machine demanding to know where Ben was and that he call her. She sounded desperate. Ben excused himself. He walked, then ran back to their flat. Allison picked up on the first ring. When she heard it was Ben she said, 'I'm pregnant.' After she said it she began to cry.

Ben returned to Boston on the next available flight. He had only his duffel bag; he left the bulk of his things in the flat with Nick. The night of his return, as he and Allison lay cramped in her bed in her dorm room, Allison, exhausted from weeping, asked, 'Why did you come back?'

Ben hesitated. In the dark he thought maybe if he didn't

answer the question would disappear. Finally he said, 'Because it's what you do.'

Beside him he felt Allison stiffen.

In the months following the abortion Ben didn't return to Dublin. 'Just hold onto my stuff,' he told Nick when he called. He contacted the provost of the college who told Ben he could withdraw without penalty from his fall courses but that he would have to attend at least as a part-time student in the spring in order to remain eligible for doctoral candidacy. Ben assured him he would be there in January and every month sent off a rent cheque to Nick on their flat.

He and Allison moved into an apartment in Brighton close to the university. They stayed home mostly. Allison didn't want anything to do with her friends or what she considered the trite and immature social environment that was college life. 'I can't stand to be around them. Things have changed for me,' she told Ben when he urged her to call one of her friends back. He told her she needed to return to her life as it was before, needed to put events behind her and move on. This led to a fight. Shouting. Allison saying, 'I can't live life the way you do, as if nothing has ever happened. I can't live like tomorrow doesn't matter.'

'Well, I'm not going to waste my time dwelling on things I can't do anything about,' Ben said.

After that, Allison stopped drinking. This wasn't a conscious decision, she merely lost the taste for it and found herself disgusted by the emotions it brought on. She didn't exercise, but lost weight from lack of eating. On the occasions when she did gorge herself, afterwards, when she thought Ben was asleep, she made herself vomit. Sometimes, without telling Ben, she went to church. When Ben questioned her, she was evasive. They fought and Allison threw a glass at him. She broke down. Crying, she told him the truth about her eating, but couldn't bring herself to use the word *bulimia*. Ben held her then, held her in his arms until well into the night.

For a while they went without fighting. They developed a routine: Ben prepared breakfast while Allison showered and got ready for classes. After she left he spent long hours of the morning lying in their bed, relieved to be alone, to feel space around him. When he did finally get up it was only to move to the couch where he read from a stack of glossy women's magazines Allison kept. In the afternoons he went to the Castelbar, an Irish pub on Washington Street. There he drank Guinness, fed money into the jukebox, played darts and engaged the bar staff and patrons in conversation just to hear their accents, lilting and melodic. When he could, he mentioned that he'd been living in Ireland. In Rathmines. That he went to UCD. Brought up the names of the few pubs he'd come to know. Then he stopped mentioning anything. Every evening, though, he was home waiting for Allison. He cooked and served their dinner and while she studied, did the dishes. When she gave up for the night, they watched TV together. They didn't talk. Ben drank whatever liquor was on hand – beer, wine, scotch, vodka – and though he never became drunk in any apparent way, he had difficulty remembering in the morning what they'd watched the night before, what they'd said to each other, what time they'd gone to bed – and all the nights became one.

In December Ben found a job at a bookstore downtown.

It was the only job he could get and the only one he thought he could tolerate. Allison dropped out of school, started work as a waitress in a bar in the Back Bay, bringing home a hundred and fifty, two hundred dollars a weekend night to Ben's six twenty-five an hour. Christmas came and went. New Year's Eve they spent at home.

On a Saturday night in January Ben went out with his fellow workers form the bookstore – most of them either putting their way through college or post-graduates like him, unsure of their next move. By midnight they'd all retired, claiming exhaustion, lack of money, work, having to catch the last T home. Alone, Ben made his way to an Irish pub, the Harp, that he knew from his time before Allison. It was a place people went looking to hook up. He tried to make eye contact with several girls, but they were all either with friends or boyfriends.

'So, why are you here alone?' a short redhead waiting for her drink at the bar asked him. She had a friendly face dashed with freckles, a smile that made him feel welcome.

Ben shrugged. He wasn't good at this. 'I don't know. I just needed to get out.'

Her name was Aisling. She told Ben to come drink with her and her friends and offered to buy him whatever he was drinking.

'Guinness.'

Aisling took his hand, introduced him. Her friends worked for an investment firm. They asked him what he did. 'I'm in grad school,' he said. 'Over the pond in Ireland.' They didn't appear interested and Ben told Aisling they should go someplace else, but she said she couldn't abandon her friends. Shortly after, she and her friends left.

'It was nice to meet you,' she told Ben.

Ben had a last pint, then took a cab to Logan airport where he sat in the same bar where six months before he'd sat with Allison. It was empty but for an unshaven traveller with his backpack on the seat beside him, flipping through a *Let's Go London.* In the waiting areas people watched television without sound, slept and occasionally, briefly, spoke. Outside the large windows the night was lit in dim orange. Ben rose and started for the Aer Lingus desk downstairs, but turned around at the bottom of the escalator and returned to the bar. The bar, though, had closed. Beyond the windows it had begun to snow.

It was past four in the morning when Ben made it back to Brighton, having walked six miles through light flurries from where he'd run out of cash for his cab fare. He discarded his wet clothes in the living room of their apartment. In the bedroom Allison flicked on the bedside lamp. Her eyes were raw and swollen from crying, her cheeks flushed. 'I thought you'd left me,' she said.

'I was at the airport.'

Allison turned to face the wall. She said, 'If you left me, Ben, it would kill me.'

Ben climbed into bed. He drew her to him but Allison shrugged him off. She said, 'Sometimes I think you don't love me any more.'

'I love you.' Ben turned off the light. In the dark he went to touch Allison's face, then withdrew his hand. 'If I didn't I wouldn't be here now.'

'You're going to leave me, aren't you?'

'I hadn't planned on it,' he joked. Then he said, 'I'll always be there for you, Allison. Believe that.'

'Is that all?'

'There's nothing more I can give.'

'Would you marry me? Some day? If things weren't what they are?'

'Yes,' Ben said.

Ben was awoken by Allison kissing his face. It was still dark; he felt groggy – not quite drunk any more, not quite hung over. When Allison saw he was awake she pulled her T-shirt off. She pressed her skin to his. He felt her on him, a bristling touch. 'Make love to me,' she said. Ben rolled her over. As he slid into her, Allison gasped. It was the first time they'd made love since before he'd left for Dublin six months before. 'Be gentle,' she whispered. 'Go slow.' They made love just as they had when they'd first fallen in love until morning brightened through the blinds and, unfinished, they fell asleep holding each other.

Later, Ben would have difficulty remembering the months that followed. His recollections of the time would consist of long silences broken by sudden, bitter arguments. Allison accusing him of abandoning her. Allison calling him a liar. Calling him selfish. Ben trying to explain something he could not find any words for. A need inside him. Once, in frustration, he slapped Allison, but eventually that, too, was added to their past. Now when they had sex it was with anger: who could control whom. Who could stay silent, take more. By degrees Ben gave up, stopped saying anything that might reveal what was in his heart.

Over Easter he visited his parents up the coast. Allison went to her mother's. Ben told her he would return to

Boston early on Monday so she wouldn't have to be alone in the apartment. They could spend the evening together.

'I think we need to concentrate on us,' Allison said.

That Monday at his parents', though, Ben found himself awake in his old bed as the world outside verged on the threshold of day. In the pre-dawn darkness everything was as it had always been: old posters of rock bands on the wall; the science fiction books he used to read lining the shelves; a second-place wrestling trophy from his sophomore year in high school. The sheets were new and fresh, but the room still held the stale odour of disuse. For a long time he lay motionless, measuring the throb of his pulse through the systems of his body. Being home made him feel as if in a timeless limbo where nothing could touch him, where there were no consequences, no responsibilities. It occurred to him that this place, in the arms of his past, was a shelter which could no longer hold him, and that the future, as he saw it with Allison, was the same: a series of these, one shelter built around another; concentric rings of safety at the centre of which survived the knowledge that he was slowly dying, as clear to him at that moment as the perfect line of shadow at the point where shadow and object touch and diverge.

This was not the life he wanted, and thinking this, he felt his heart harden.

On the way back to Boston he drove as if nothing had changed; just like any other day returning home. He tried to keep his mind empty. They were lucky enough to have a parking space behind their apartment. He left his car there. Without going into the apartment he walked to Commonwealth Avenue and hailed a taxi.

'Logan,' he said. 'International terminal.'

At the Aer Lingus desk he used the return portion of his ticket from Dublin to get himself a seat on the next flight to Ireland. The ticket had spent the last seven months tucked inside his passport in a side pocket of his knapsack. Even at the last a part of him hoped the passport wouldn't be there or the airline wouldn't honour the ticket or that there wouldn't be a flight that day. A part of him, the frightened part, hoped not to go through with this.

'Enjoy your trip,' the woman behind the counter said as she handed back his passport along with his boarding pass.

Six hours later the plane landed at Shannon airport on the west coast of Ireland. It was early in the morning, Irish time. According to Ben's watch it was just after midnight. On a whim he disembarked at Shannon instead of continuing on to Dublin as planned; there was nothing for him in Dublin, he was too late for school and hadn't written to Nick since before Christmas. After clearing customs with only his small knapsack he stepped out of the airport doors onto the empty access road that led through the green countryside in the direction of Limerick. He didn't feel the relief he'd anticipated, though. With no other choice he started down the road. He turned when a car approached from behind and stuck out his thumb for a ride.

'Where you heading?' the driver asked.

'Wherever you're going is fine.'

He had three more rides that day. The last dropped him at the Cliffs of Moher on the west coast of the island between the gaping mouth of the River Shannon and Galway Bay. 'They're worth having a look,' the driver, a middle-aged man on his way to Galway City, said. 'If you want, I'll wait.' Ben told him it wouldn't be necessary.

From the lip of the cliffs, the surf silent on the rocks eight hundred feet below, Ben stared unfocused into the air across the ocean as if he might make out another shore there. As evening rose out of the east in balance to the sinking sun, he descended the winding road to the fishing village nestled in the shadows of the cliffs. *Doolin*, read the name in black on a white signpost. At the only pub in town, O'Connor's, he drank one pint after another and listened to the musicians gathered in the corner, lost and happy for a moment, ignoring the fact he hadn't slept, until he knew he could avoid the inevitable no longer. He stepped out into the empty, ill-lit street to a phone booth and from there called Allison.

He imagined their apartment. A rectangle of dying sunlight narrowing on the floor, becoming a sliver of white up the wall, then a flare swallowed by the shadows of the afternoon. The dust that had hung suspended and distinct, almost tangible in it, disappearing. Allison lifting the receiver, holding it between her fingers as she would an hors d'oeuvre. Only the white, bloodless tips of her fingers betraying any strain.

'Hello?'

He would remember looking at his reflection in the glass of the booth, his skin ashen, the whites of his eyes glazed a shade of red. 'It's me, Allison.'

'Where the fuck are you? I've been worried sick.'

'I'm in Ireland. I'm calling from Ireland.'

Silence.

Much of what followed Ben would only remember in snippets. Him saying he'd had a vision: the two of them eating dinner together the way they always did, watching TV, going to sleep, going to work. Allison saying, 'And what's wrong with that? Are you better than that?' Trying to explain how he was scared of something moving away faster than he could hold on; Allison asking, what about her, what was she supposed to do? Saying, 'You came back to me, Ben. When you were away, you came back. You said that was more important to you than anything.' Saying, 'This isn't you.' Mostly, though, they hung on in silence, the only sound the barely perceptible presence of the phone line between them. Ben imagined Allison on the other end flicking through the channels on the television with the remote, the muted images passing too quick to catch.

'I feel so old,' Allison said. 'Weren't we young once? Weren't we happy together? In love? We could start again. I make enough money. You can go to school. We can do it all right. We always said we would be the ones, we would make it through. You and me.'

Ben thought of all the things he could say. Here was his opportunity. What followed, though, carried the uncontrollable force of inevitability: 'I'm not going back to school,' he said. Then, pressed by the silence, 'I'm not in Dublin, Allison. I'm in a phone booth in a village on the coast.'

'Jesus, Ben.'

'What?'

'That's the best you can come up with? "What?" And you call yourself an English major? Fuck you, Ben . . .'

Maybe it was the distance. Ben was surprised at how easy it felt to say nothing, to shut everything off so it couldn't touch him. He waited only for the quiet to close in. Hold him. 'I don't understand you,' Allison said. She'd begun to cry. 'You came back. You said you'd always be here for me, that you'd never leave me. That's what you said.' It was like he wasn't there any more, like he was witness to her anguish only through the connection of the phone line.

'How can you just say nothing? Doesn't this mean anything to you?'

Ben was quiet. Not even the silence could create words that weren't inside him.

'Part of you has always been looking past me. From the first time you kissed me and told me you loved me, I knew you'd abandon me. I knew it, but I'm just a stupid girl. God, I'm stupid. Stupid, stupid, stupid. Well, Ben, I guess you did your bit. You came back when you had to, now your job is done. You can go. Go ahead. Happy? You're free. That's what you want, isn't it? But I want you to know, we had a baby, Ben. I was pregnant with your child. We were that close. Don't you understand that?' Ben felt cold. He drew his arm around himself. 'You can't just let go. I thought you learned that. Something has to survive this. It has to, Ben. It has to.'

Down the street from Ben the door to the pub opened and for a moment there escaped the din of voices and music. A man stepped out smoking a cigarette. He paused as the door shut behind him, then lurched in Ben's direction. An old man in a rumpled suit the colour of earth, his waistcoat buttoned but for the bottom button, his tie tight and thickly knotted, a hat on his head. He passed the booth with a nod and started up the grassy hill that rose on the opposite side of the street where Ben until then had seen no path.

'I'll always love you, Allison,' he tried, but his words held no promise.

'Don't speak to me of love. This isn't love. You don't love me. You used to love me. You're heart was mine once, Ben. You opened it to me. You adored me. You worshipped me. You told me we were like nothing else on this earth. You said I was everything to you. Remember how we used to talk, the things we used to say? Such beautiful, beautiful words. Or were those only words, Ben? Was it all only words?'

Ben looked at the hill where the man had begun his ascent. He would later think that it was words that got you in trouble. It was words that distorted the truth. So easy to manipulate, wind around the tongue, create from them a person behind whom you could hide until there wasn't anything left of you.

'You've taken everything from me, you bastard,' Allison said, crying. 'You don't know what I want to do to you. I want to hurt you. But you've taken even that, you bastard. How can I touch you; I can't even see you? It's like you're not real.' She stopped. Across the line Ben could make out only faintly the sound of her breathing as it barely ruffled the silence so vast and clear around him that he felt like he was underwater. He leaned his body against the glass door of the booth. He heard Allison as from out of a hole, her voice a peep. Saying that they weren't even people any more. They were spirits. Ghosts. Saying there was no hope for ghosts; they were dead.

Part Three
A HAPPINESS DEEP AND TWISTED

In Your Blood

So this is what happens: you get into a fight. For *singing*. There you are coming home from a night out with your buddies at one in the morning on a subway platform downtown belting your song across the tracks and down the tunnel. You're happy, you're married and in nine months you'll be a father – that's what has you singing. Turns out, though, this guy in a suit with his tie undone takes offence and starts talking trash: what are you, fucked? What the fuck is that shit? Shut your hole with that crap.

You're drunk. You say something back, doesn't matter what. Anything. The guy in the suit gets pissed off, draws close. He's loaded. He doesn't just swing at you but starts in pounding – his fist to your face, fist to face. You're bleeding, can taste it in your mouth. You're seeing white and red and this guy in the suit keeps at it: jab, jab, upper cut. He doesn't even have blood on his suit. Somehow you manage to get him in a bear hug and start landing a couple of your own. Little rabbit punches to the kidneys. Just a couple more, he's starting to feel 'em. You know it. You're young. You're drunk. You can take him.

As it happens, though, this fucker, this stockbroker in his

pinstriped suit, has a knife on him. A butterfly knife he whips around his wrist. You don't feel him cut you but you can tell you're bleeding from your ribs and you've pissed in your pants. You can't help it. It's what happens.

When the cops come they don't see this and cuff the both of you. There's no way you can be cut bad, they tell you, because what they saw when they arrived was you breaking the guy's jaw with your skull and him crying and holding his hands over his face. And you standing. But you don't remember this. You don't know where it came from. All you remember is a blinding whiteness after he stabbed you and no pain and a fury you didn't want to control. That must've been when you cracked him in the face with your head.

The cops take you to the hospital in the cruiser. The other guy gets an ambulance. You try to tell them he's the one who had the knife, he's the one who stabbed you first, but it's you they saw standing and when they take the corners they turn hard so you slam against the window. You stopped bleeding a long time ago, another mistake, so they take the long way. Tell you you shouldn't have messed with a stockbroker carrying a knife. Boxer, too, says the other one. The cops laugh.

At the hospital the attending tells the cops to uncuff you and gives them an earful for not calling an ambulance. You feel like a kid again, counting on the good graces of the only teacher smart enough to recognize that right and wrong are tenuous abstractions. But the attending doesn't care about right and wrong, doesn't differentiate – sees an injury and goes to treat it. You admire this lack of judgment, wish you had it yourself.

The cops they just shrug it off. What's it to them?

When you're stitched up and bandaged it's off to the precinct. They're joking, tell you next time you shouldn't leave yourself exposed like that, tell you the guy who cut you is the son of the DA. They don't like the DA and don't like his son, they say, but they don't seem to like you either.

At the station things happen fast. There's a moment of deliberation between the two arresting officers, then it's Felony Assault. Shouldn't have been fighting on city property, they say. They shrug. It's out of their hands. Other guy should get the same, probably, they say.

Mysteriously, though, the other guy's charges – the boxer, the DA's son, the knife-carrying stockbroker – his charges get dropped. Just as mysteriously you've suddenly got a record, something about Assault and Battery trumped up out of a fight you somehow got involved in back in college over a girl who fucked you over. Then there's a drug charge you know nothing about and a night in the drunk tank. You begin to wonder what country you're in. You tell your lawyer none of this happened, but all he can do is shake his head and mention Kafka.

Kafka, my ass, you say, this is impossible. This isn't supposed to happen.

But this is the way it's happening.

Eventually you calm down, assured this will never go to trial. The judge, he'll throw it out. Nothing to worry about, but you're thinking this is bullshit. You consider yourself a fighter. You won't back down. You're not proud of what happened, but at least you didn't back down. You took him to the count. For what it's worth, which isn't much.

Consider yourself lucky to have landed the woman who is now your wife. She has a way of touching you that's all comfort. She doesn't ask any questions, doesn't need explanations, and that's love to you. It's so much love you made her pregnant and it didn't scare you and you know now, what's to be scared of? Nights, you feel safer thinking about her, thinking about the kid whose father you are to be. She tells you not to worry, everything will work out; by the time the child is born all this will be over, done. She says it's sure not to go to court. She says she knows this isn't you; she loves you no matter what, and you want to cry. You're so happy to have her you want to cry, because that's what love will do to a man.

But then the lawyers start talking jail-time. Seven to twelve years. You're going to court – no plea bargain, no settlement. You want to settle, the assistant DA says, Plead Guilty.

Your lawyer tells you he doesn't know what's going on. He's just a third year law student; this is way out of his hands. He expected a simple assault case – good experience. He has finals to study for, the Bar.

At your arraignment he and the assistant DA start shouting at each other. The assistant DA, a woman in her thirties with hard wrinkles around her lips that make her look like a terrier, goes red in the face. Red through and through. You've been sitting in the courtroom two days now and seen nothing: petty theft, thirty days. Public intoxication, small fine. Next. Next. Nothing, until you're up. You wonder what this woman has against you. You wonder what you represent to her. What is it she hates that you must be made an example of?

Sidebar, the judge shouts, slamming his gavel. What is this, a fucking movie?

You watch. You try to listen. It's in his blood, you're sure you hear the assistant DA say. Then it's over. Emerging from the huddle you see her smiling. Your lawyer looks sheepish. The judge makes a motion like the raising of his palms, tied by the law. State wants to prosecute, state prosecutes.

Nothing we can do, your lawyer tells you. Plead guilty or go to trial. You'll probably be acquitted, but the way things are going I can't guarantee it. Can't guarantee anything. You could get seven to twelve.

Seven to twelve. It shouldn't happen, but then things shouldn't even have come to this. You shouldn't be going to trial. Seven to twelve. You'll be thirty-five when you get out, at the youngest. Plead guilty and it's three years, two with good behaviour. For being stabbed. For singing. You can't even remember why you were singing. Or what. You can't trust your perceptions any more. Who are you now? A husband, a soon-to-be father. Sooner than that, a convict. Plead guilty and come out a felon. Fill out an application and where it asks if you've ever been convicted of a felony – well, you know the answer. That's what you are. A felon.

What you're thinking, though, you're thinking you have a kid on the way. You're going to be a father. What are you going to do? See him on visits for the next seven to twelve years, try to explain to him why the other kids don't need to come here to see their pop? You think of everything you'll miss. Or you could plead guilty. You could be out before your child's second birthday, that's what you could do for your child. Sacrifice your freedom. The answer is obvious.

So it's agreed, you plead guilty. No trial. The assistant DA smiles. Your lawyer is off studying for the Bar; his professor has taken over the case and worries about the precedent being set. You never even saw the DA. His son, you hear, is back working at the brokerage house, his jaw wired shut for the next eight weeks. You hear he's clearing two hundred grand a year, probably more. But he's not talking. You find this out through a friend from college who works down in the Financial District.

Well, you do your time and you don't really want to talk about it. What's to talk about? You were in a general security lock-up at the hour of your son's birth. You missed his first steps, his first words, but you've got all the rest. You spend a lot of time consoling yourself in the love of your child. You watch him and feel love. Unconditional love. But there are times still when you get angry at the forces that stole two years of your life away from you. Your son's birth, his presence – they can't erase that. When you watch him you pray to yourself that one day you won't have this anger inside you any more. You pray he won't see through the façade of good cheer you have going. More than anything you pray he won't ever come to witness this anger. You pray every night after you've put him to bed and watch him in slumber that he will never test it.

The thought scares you. A thought you won't tell your wife, his mother. She would tear your heart out for having it. For merely letting it surface. It *is* true, though: the possibility exists that your son will one day drive in at that spot of anger, as the possibility exists for anything to happen – and, remembering the searing whiteness during which you broke another man's jaw with your skull, you swear to yourself you will be a gentle man. And you hope that this too may be true.

A Long Way from Skagway

Mud season, and Francis got it into his head he needed to head west. For a week now he'd been sitting on his bed in his lightless studio apartment drinking red wine and talking to himself.

'Control,' he told himself. 'Get a grip.'

Until two weeks ago he'd worked at setting up and running web sites but had since quit any efforts at production owing to an inexplicable tension pulling on his skull and knotting at the top of his spine. He tried aspirin, ibuprofen, Tylenol, even some codeine left over from an old prescription. The only thing that seemed to help was red wine. Today was the worst yet. He tried to go for a walk, but even in the rain the grey-green light stung his eyes so badly he had to squeeze them shut behind his sunglasses and return home like a blind man.

This is a bad one, he thought. 'See your way through it, Francis. Suck it up.'

Ten days before Francis had stopped talking to people and on Monday had without any explanation told Kathy, his girlfriend of the last year, it would be best to avoid him. She'd been nonplussed. He didn't want her to see him when he began to lose it for real. God only knew what he might do. Foreseeable as hurricane season down in Florida, where he'd lived before moving to the starker confines of the New England coast, these dark funks were as unpredictable in their nature, intensity and path as the storms that rolled off the sea and battered the shore.

He'd picked up the habit in Florida, naming his bouts the way they did hurricanes. The opposite of hurricane season, though, they usually hit near the end of winter, just when the sunlight hours began again to consume the day, but long before the first shoots poked out of their leafy shells in anticipation of summer.

In the past he'd taken a series of flights around the world, flying off to wherever was cheapest. Hundred bucks to London; two hundred to Rio. At each airport he called for the next flight out, didn't matter where as long as it left soon and didn't cost much. In this way he circumnavigated the globe, touching down on all the continents without ever actually leaving an airport. That had been during Harold. A bad one. Ellen had him moving by train through Europe, where spring came earlier, searching out the most perfect cafés to sit at and view the world from. During Benedict he'd taken a Greyhound bus to Miami where he watched the models strut along South Beach. Once he even made it to Everest Base Camp at seventeen thousand feet just to see that hunk of a mountain. That was in the throes of Jeremiah.

This year he'd go west. He'd never been to the other coast, never seen the sun set on an ocean as vast as the Pacific. I-90 straight across, he figured. Stay at his brother's in Wisconsin, then through the Dakota Badlands, maybe stop at Mount Rushmore, through Wyoming, Montana, Idaho, Washington State. From there a ferry ran up the coast from Seattle to Skagway, Alaska, a one-road town popular on the cruise ship circuit and with summer back-packers living out of their tents. So he'd read in a travel guide. This time of year there'd still be plenty of snow, though now the spring equinox had passed and with Skagway so far north, the days would be a touch longer.

Before doubt could get its claws into him, he was up. He felt giddy. Matilda: that's what he'd call this one.

Half an hour later he had a small duffel bag packed and was heading south to I-90. From there the western part of the state passed without a problem. Despite the rain washing away what remained of the dirty, crumbly snow on the hillsides, he felt good. Better than he had in ages. A touch euphoric even. Maybe this was all he needed, a high-speed drive through the country in the middle of the week. Maybe he could find a lonesome Bed and Breakfast, call Kathy, have her drive out. They could do all the things you were supposed to do. He laughed. For the first time in he didn't know how long, he became aroused. *The new, improved me,* he thought. *Tabula rasa.*

The sensation was fleeting, though, and once through Albany an ugliness descended on him. The notion struck that he could as easily swing his car into the support pillar of an overpass as hold the road. It wouldn't be hard, a quick jerk on the wheel at the right moment. That's all there was to it. So easy. He turned up the radio, opened the window a crack. No good. On either side of the highway stretched hard, rubbly farmland. It could bring the best of men down:

rocky, shrunken plots; farmhouses in need of new doors, new roofs, a paint job; cars on blocks in the driveway.

He wondered what Kathy was doing then. Working on her boat? Getting ready to sail away from him? Maybe he should've called her before he left, shouldn't have said what he did about avoiding him. Maybe even proposed to her. He came up with adjectives: sweet, charitable, attentive, sensuous, intelligent, matter-of-fact. Very much in touch with her emotions, her desires. Perfect, really. She'd never seen him in one of his funks, though.

In the last months he'd withdrawn almost completely inside himself. Walking by himself. Reading Baudelaire's *Flowers of Evil*. Feigning sleep whenever Kathy wanted to talk or make love, shying from her touch. All winter long, whenever she was around, his thoughts had turned to disappearing and being invisible and he couldn't get himself aroused except when alone. Occasionally his thoughts turned darker: suicide; rage; the idea of murder and rape and the bone-chilling knowledge these might not be beyond him. Kathy never said a thing. When he'd suggested she avoid him she'd responded with only the slightest nod and a shifting of her eyes. Her only acknowledgment came when she'd suddenly clutched herself to him in the middle of the night two weeks ago and told him everything would be OK. What she'd meant by 'everything', he didn't know.

Francis, seeing he was nearly out of gas, pulled into a rest area. After filling up he called Kathy's number at work, the only place she was reachable, then hung up. Kathy, he reminded himself, was herself a little loopy and not always the easiest cookie to chew on. She'd been in law school when her husband of two years left her. She finished her degree, then soloed her father's thirty-six-foot ketch from Boothbay Harbor, Maine, to Perth, Australia, where she married a surfer – a purely selfish act of convenience, in her words, that allowed her to stay and work on the butt end of the world, away from all the troubles and anxieties that had driven her to sea in the first place. There she spent several years running her boat as a charter, among other things. He hoped that in the strange way they had, she would understand he didn't really have a choice about what he was now doing.

On the road again, a manic lightness took hold of Francis. Maybe it was the isolation of driving. The sense of resignation. Freedom. Whatever it was, he swung off his set course in the direction of Niagara Falls where he spent half an hour standing in the drizzle trying to follow a single spot of water as it slipped over the edge and dropped into the mist that rose from the base. He repeated the effort again and again, lost in the white, frothy tumble and the roar of water. For a moment he considered jumping into that roar, got so far as to climb over the rail and step onto a suitable perch before stopping, a sheen of sweat mixing with the mist clinging to his skin.

'Maybe we should go,' he said aloud.

'Good idea,' he answered.

From Niagara he drove north past Toronto, shaken by the possibility of his having jumped. It was as close as he'd ever come to testing his existence like that.

Over and around Lake Huron and the Georgian Bay the highway turned into a single-lane road. Flat pine forest stretched left and right. He passed communities so small their only demarcations were a single gas pump in front of a grocery-store-cum-post-office-cum-tavern. Eventually the sun set, leaving nothing to see but the occasional set of oncoming headlights.

This was when the first hallucinations hit: a blow-up dummy in the passenger seat that looked like Kathy. She was trying to speak. 'Don't think; just experience,' it sounded like. When he looked he found the seat empty and had to remind himself he was alone. As soon as he returned his eyes to the road, there was his brother, Jess, drinking a beer, poking fun at Francis's anxiety. 'You're wigging, bro. I wish I could be as paranoid as you.' Francis dared not turn for fear Jess too would disappear. Except Jess was off in Arizona on a solo hike through the Grand Canyon's backcountry. And Kathy was in Massachusetts. Or else at sea. It wasn't paranoid to think she had left him.

The radio said, 'The beginning of all knowledge is ignorance. The beginning of all polish is diligence.'

Fucking Matilda. Francis shook his head, squeezed his eyes shut. To focus himself he calculated the mileage he'd been making. His average speed. What that came to in kilometres per hour. How far he could push the needle before having to gas up again. When the moon, diffuse through the cloud cover, rose near full over the horizon he turned off the headlights and drove by the dim glow cast on the barren landscape. The trees had disappeared, replaced by a rocky terrain he couldn't for the life of him account for unless this was another hallucination. It was as if the skin and flesh of the earth had been seared away in a single furious blast. He opened the window. Convinced he couldn't be asleep, he assumed this barren, blasted vision was another creation of his tweaked psyche, but the terrain continued, ignoring his efforts at clearing his mind. Finally he pulled his car over.

He stepped out and began walking. The rock beneath his feet felt like glass. He was afraid to touch it and find out it was. Ahead lay nothing but more smooth, undulating stone. Gathering his courage he bent down, brushed his hand against the surface. Moss, slick with moisture and freezing now with the dropping temperature. He rubbed his hands. Here and there he made out what he hoped were stunted, leafless trees and not people watching him silently from the dark. He turned to find the road but couldn't see his car. He shivered, rubbed his hands some more. From over the next rise there came a slight shimmer against the mist. Perhaps this was all illusion, nothing more – but when he made the rise he saw that the glow emanated from some distant community. The mining town of Sudbury, he figured. He realized he was standing smack dab in the middle of what had at one point been hard-core strip-mining country. There had once been forest here. This damaged land, brutalized, bitter in shape, mean in disposition, with no hint of generosity. He turned back, first walking, then running. Running hard to make the road. When he spotted his car he sprinted. Once inside he flared the high beams, locked the doors, and turned up the radio.

'Holy Jesus.' So this was how it was going to be.

Eleven months before, in the full force of Luther, Francis had done this bit where he ditched his apartment and junked most of his possessions, keeping only what he could fit in his car. He lived out of his car for almost three months,

still going to his job at the software company. It was while
heavily into Luther that he met Kathy; about the time he felt
sure he'd never return to a normal, homebound existence.
He'd taken a liking to the minimalist aspects of his new life.
It kept costs down, and he felt less bound. Then there was
his idea of reaching a state of continuous motion while still
existing within the confines of a given space.

One night at the bar Francis frequented Kathy approached him. Having recently brought her boat back from
Australia she had the look of determination and of the sea,
her long hair bleached by salt and sun, her body tanned, her
muscles taut. He noticed tiny, soft freckles dotting her lips
and wanted to feel their invisible touch. She had a slight
Aussie accent when she told him that she'd never approached a man before. She said she'd noticed his hands.
They looked tender. Her own, Francis noticed, seemed
strong.

An hour later Kathy suggested they leave, maybe go
someplace, so Francis drove her along the coast and
eventually parked at a place where they could see the ocean
and hear the crash of waves.

'Is this where we start heavy petting?' Kathy laughed.
'Should we go to the back seat?'

'This is where I live.' It suddenly struck Francis as silly.
'Actually, I usually park over behind those trees out of sight
of the cops so I don't get bothered, but this is it. This is my
place. Would you prefer I drive you home now?'

'You live in your car? Here?'

He'd had in mind a stoic, silent routine, but suddenly
Francis found himself telling Kathy about his attempt at

unencumbered existence, trying to live in tandem with society without actually having to remove himself.

'So, has it worked?'

'Not really.' He laughed. 'But I've grown used to it.'

'So, what do you think?' Kathy smiled.

'What?'

'I'd like to try it.'

They spent nine days in his car driving up and down the New England coast, sleeping in the back seat, eating on the hood, having sex any which way they could find room. He skipped out on his job. When they began to wonder about what to do next Kathy suggested he move in with her. So he did, onto her boat. That lasted through the summer. His old boss offered him a raise to come back, which he did for a while, but then he quit for good, got the studio as a place to work out of and started in on his web programming business. Eventually he moved in. Kathy in the meantime got a job handling accounts at a boat manufacturer down the coast in Massachusetts and stayed living on her boat. She said she liked the rock of the water beneath her.

Now six months later, in Sudbury, Canada, Francis parked in a truck stop and once again sat fitfully in his car, huddled in the driver's seat with his sleeping bag wrapped around him, waiting for sleep to hurry the dawn along, hoping his dreams would readily separate themselves from reality.

By the time the first touches of grey washed the sky Francis was on the road again, having slept only intermittently. At one point he'd felt sure he was standing watch on Kathy's boat and that the wind knocking against the car was actually the sway of the water beneath. He'd been convinced they were out at sea, Kathy below deck while he, roped in, manned the wheel.

Within a couple of hours Francis hit the US-Canadian border between Lake Huron and Lake Superior. He flirted with the idea of turning north to Thunder Bay, but decided to try for his original course, heading down to Milwaukee and over the Madison where he could crash the night in Jess's apartment, then in the morning catch up with I-90 again. As he entered Madison, though, and crossed the causeway that ran between Lake Monona and Monona Bay, despite their being frozen and not a palm tree in sight, he found himself on one of the long bridges that stretched over the ocean from the Florida mainland to Key West. He remembered nights spent drinking beer with Jess in their hammocks on his front porch, looking out over the water and dreaming up future adventures, including going to Alaska together. They were like twins, he sometimes thought, two halves of a whole. He missed his brother's company, especially now, and longed for the easy rapport they shared. So, within sight of Jess's apartment, Francis swung his car around and returned to the highway where, instead of heading north on 90, he made his way south to I-80, the idea being to get to Las Vegas about the same time Jess returned from the Canyon. It was as good a plan as any. As good as Skagway.

Once in Iowa the weather took on a strange quality, a combination of sudden snow squalls and blinding sunlight. Francis had to squint to make out the lines of the highway while all around, the countryside lay bathed in white brilliance. The wind, coming in gusts, threatened to jerk him off the road or send him into a spin. The car fishtailed: right, then left, then back again. Passing vehicles blared their horns, swerved off the road, coasted by. Francis tried to bring his under control, but any nudge of the wheel sent the car's rear in an even greater arc until it swung in one, then two, full circles before coming to a stop facing the oncoming traffic. He focused in time to see an eighteen wheeler bearing down on him. The truck's trailer swung back and forth as the driver hit the brakes. Its horn blared. A car squeezed past, another slowed to avoid being swept off the road by the penduluming of the trailer. A station wagon went into its own three-sixty. Time slowed, almost stopped, the way they said, then – voom, the truck barrelled past. Its trailer, miraculously, swung in the opposite direction away from Francis.

In his rear-view mirror he caught sight of the trucker slowly regaining control of his rig, narrowing the arc of the trailer until it once again followed behind him. The other cars on the highway resumed their progress. Drivers stared out their windows at Francis. His was the only vehicle stopped. He was sweating, running his fingers through his hair, breathing.

'Shit,' he muttered. 'Shit.'

On the plains outside Denver, so flat it felt like driving in circles around the horizon, Francis pulled into a Motel 6. He showered, then lay on the neatly made bed, reluctant to disturb the covers. He watched cable, drank a couple of beers, switched to scotch. He thought of calling Kathy, but wasn't sure what he would say. He wasn't prepared for a lengthy conversation about how he could just take off without notice or warning. Nor was he prepared for the possibility of her nonchalance. What if she simply said, 'Yeah, sure, call me when you get back?' While he'd spent most of his life trying to fit – in his own weird way – into the workings of the normal, workaday world, even forcing himself to read the sports pages in order to better shoot the breeze at the bar or the water cooler or on his doorstep, Kathy wanted no part of the quotidian and aggressively sought to break barriers. It could be she was right then planning her return to Australia where she'd left behind what she always referred to as 'a brilliant situation' while he dallied here in a motel at the foot of the Rockies dwelling on the pointlessness of existence and his inability to trust.

Sometime closer to dawn than midnight, while watching a soft-porn movie on Pay Per View he spent six dollars for, a beer in his lap, Francis glanced out the window of his room. He wanted to be sure no one was trying to break in. Across the highway an abandoned car sat in the far breakdown lane, flames consuming it from hood to trunk. He saw no obvious clues as to why. No signs of an accident; nor of anyone who might be the owner.

Occasionally a car passed, slowed, then sped on. He expected to see a police cruiser or a fire truck, but none showed and he wondered if he should call 911. He didn't, and for a long time he watched the car burn until all that remained was the blackened husk of its body. In the morning when he looked out the window after only a few hours of furtive shut-eye he found no evidence of the car, no remains, no soot marks on the tar even, and it occurred to him it could have either been a dream so visceral it felt real or else another hallucination. Either way it frightened him. His heart thumping a tight, syncopated rhythm against his ribs, he gathered his things and dropped his room key in the deposit box. Once on the highway he floored the accelerator. He aimed for the snowy mountains ahead, black and silver in the sunlight, where he hoped the scenery might somehow distract him. All the while he tried to convince himself he wasn't losing his mind, rationalizing that anyone capable of observing himself going mad had to in fact be sane.

'Get a grip, Francis,' he muttered. 'Deal with it.'

Later he muttered, 'Be good to me, Matilda. Be good to me.'

Despite his hopes, the mountains rising young and furious from the plains did nothing to make him feel any less like a pinball careening around an arcade machine and he found himself remembering what Kathy had said about her time in Australia, how in the aftermath of her wrecked marriage she'd 'enjoyed the benefits of being an attractive female pilot on charters that were a lot of times mostly male'. This despite her marriage to the surfer. 'It was empowering,' she said.

And there it was: he didn't trust her. Didn't trust anyone, and especially not himself.

The first time he and Kathy made love, half-clothed in the passenger seat of his car, Kathy's feet on the dash, his knee hard against the gearshift, the windows steamed from their body heat, Kathy had interrupted their fumble of hands and necessary body parts to tell him dry as gin that she was actually a Born Again Virgin: six months at sea and some time since had wiped the slate clean. He'd laughed; but the knowledge existed that there was nothing holding either of them. Such was the nature of their relationship: one of no attachments, of the moment. Free to do what they wanted. Fuck who they chose. Come and go as they pleased. They had nothing to go on, no commitment, no promises, not even the word *love*. Just faith.

Around Christmas when the first touches of agitation began poking at his tender spots, Francis had two drunken flings in close succession. Neither amounted to much, the first ending after only a few kisses when the girl, a waitress putting herself through college, changed her mind and gave him the brush-off. The second might actually have gone to its promised conclusion had he not been too drunk to stand and passed out with his head on her stomach. Maybe it was a kind of self-defence. He never told Kathy, but assumed she knew, that she could tell and chose not to say anything. Despite the list of everything else he'd tried in his life he'd never cheated on anyone. He'd felt sullied and wondered, wondered still, what it would take to be born again a virgin – to have the experience, the notch on the belt, and at the same time have it count for nothing. It seemed so easy on the surface. But experience left him feeling used. Like when he'd been a kid and sought out the body of a neighbour, dead from a stroke in his back yard, before police and ambulances arrived. There were some things you shouldn't see or do unless you had to.

Emerging from the mountains in time with the spreading pink sunset Francis was struck by the landscape, its rough crags dusted by snow, its sweeping expanse of open sky, the stinging brightness of the dying sun and dryness of the air.

He was amazed this country existed at all and was in immediate awe of the uncaring dominance the land held here. Cruising along the empty highway he checked the gas gauge again and again to be sure he wouldn't end up stranded. This was a place where mistakes cost dearly. Where existence had heft and weight. He wondered how Jess was managing alone out in the Canyon. People, he knew, died there every year.

As soon as the sun dropped away the temperature plummeted. The Utah desert disappeared. The last few hours had gone well, but Francis felt the strain of driving: hands, elbows, ankles and thighs sore from being in the same position three days now. Time became distorted, non-existent. It occurred to him he hadn't had a thought in he didn't know how long. Just an emptiness. Like flying straight through the heart of nothing. He didn't want to lose the feeling and figured he could be in Las Vegas well before midnight. But after checking the clock on the car's dash a couple of times he discovered it had stopped. At the same time the visions returned, stronger this time: colours and amorphous shapes out of the corners of his eyes at first, then straight on hallucinations: a pterodactyl swooping from the sky; a wolf or coyote running alongside his car at ninety miles an hour; Kathy, in white, wet with rain, standing by the road hitching a ride, shouting, 'Catch me if you can.' He locked his brakes and slowed almost to a stop before she disappeared. He tried to laugh but didn't have it in him. He opened the window to check for rain. None. Of course not, this was the desert. The air was cold, dry. He left the window open to let the air wash over him. More than a few times he found himself driving in the gravel beside the road or across the yellow lines. Beyond the point of questioning, Francis gripped the wheel tighter and kept his eyes on the spot where the headlights hit the tar. Like that, white-knuckled, breathing heavy, sweating, he made it through the gauntlet of worsening hallucinations – clouds mistaken for mountains, the desert for sea; a roar in his ears like a low-flying jet when there was only empty sky bleached by moonlight; the sound of a gull; and again Kathy on the side of the road – and arrived in Las Vegas.

Most obvious about Las Vegas was that it was open twenty-four-seven. A place where the days of the week didn't matter, where night and day were the same, located in a desert without seasons, where the only currency was cash and anything could be purchased.

As he swooped through the low hills that surrounded the city, shrouded in a veil of dust swept up by the wind, Francis made out first a hotel in the shape of the New York skyline, then one in that of a giant pyramid, and he wondered if this wasn't just another hallucination. After twice driving the length of the neon-lit strip with its advertisements for cheap food, five cent slots, one dollar blackjack, topless reviews, Ice Capades, animal shows and any number of other entertainments, Francis pulled into one of the few hotels without a casino. He remembered Jess mentioning it. On the off chance he might show, Francis left a message with the front desk. He imagined his brother's unsurprised reaction as he read the note. A slight shrug, maybe a shaking of the head.

Once in his room Francis fell on the bed and opened a warm beer. He hoped he would be lucky enough to run into his brother, if only to hear a voice he would recognize as similar to his own. Though now he thought about it he might be completely off on the name of the hotel, and for that matter the tentative date of Jess's return.

He lay on the bed only a few minutes before restlessness took him and he ventured out onto the strip. The wind had grown worse, but he didn't have to walk far, just across the street to a large casino whose name he didn't notice. As he stepped through the door, banks of slot machines confronted him. No reception, no information desk, no way to reference himself. The world outside disappeared. Francis plunged a quarter into the closest machine hoping an air of indifference would bring him luck. Nothing. His third quarter, though, won him fifty in return and with this he managed to pass the next hour moving from one machine to the next, accepting drinks from the long-legged cocktail waitresses working the room.

Eventually he graduated to five- and ten-dollar blackjack tables, roulette, craps. He increased his bets and four times had to withdraw money from a cash machine until he was sure he was well into the realm of overdraft protection. *Fuck it.* The activity of continually trying to redeem his growing losses kept his mind off other thoughts – such as what exactly he was doing here in Las Vegas, no closer to Skagway and now just as far from home, and what had become of Kathy.

'Jesus.' He shook his head. *Matilda.* Was this the calm, the centre, the eye?

As he put a hundred dollars on red at the roulette table a tall woman with long blonde hair, obviously fake breasts and a face cast into perfection by the careful application of make-up sidled up beside him. She smiled and he smiled back. She was dressed in an elegant but short and tight-fitting black dress. It didn't take long to peg her as a hooker.

'Hi,' she said. 'My name's Loretta.'

'Francis.'

'Francis. That's a nice name.'

Together they watched the roulette wheel go into motion. They didn't speak. Kept their eyes on the ball, waiting for it to drop from its orbit and bounce into place. Before Francis could even register that he'd lost, his money had been swept away.

'This is a tough town. Maybe you'll have more luck with love,' Loretta said. 'Would you like to go somewhere?'

Francis put another hundred dollars down, this time on a specific number. Again they waited. He understood immediately he'd lost and said, 'Sure.'

They sat at one of the bars. Before a silence could develop Loretta started on about Texas, where she'd been raised. Everything was better in Texas. It was a place, she said, where people were real. Where you could trust a person. Francis, only half listening, wondered where the hell he was from. He'd been to and lived in so many places it didn't matter. And what was real? What did it mean to be a *real* person? Was he one? *To thine own self be true,* he thought. There was Kathy, her promiscuous charters, the strange fact she could only come at sea, the reputation she was sure to have had. Did that make her more real? Less? He remembered the story Kathy had told him about cheating on her first husband, the one she thought was her true love, her happily-ever-after until he left her; how right after their engagement, while home from college, she sneaked into another guy's bed and had sex with him. Just the once. Just to see what another man would feel like. He'd admired her for that – still did. Was that what it meant to be real?

'So, what are you doing in Vegas?' Loretta asked. 'Here to gamble?'

'I'm on my way to Skagway.'

'Where's that?'

'Alaska.'

She laughed. 'Well, you're a long way from Skagway, let me tell you.'

'I know.'

'A long way.' She laughed again, drawing out the word *long*.

Francis paid the tab and they left. Outside the wind had risen and flung giant handfuls of fine sand through the air, over the tarmac, into billboards. Cars used their wipers to clear their windshields; pedestrians bent their heads to protect their eyes. Crossing the street, Loretta and Francis walked side by side against the onslaught.

In the parking lot of the hotel, where the wind didn't come as hard, Loretta asked, 'Are you all right? You don't really look . . .'

'I don't really know,' Francis said.

For some reason he didn't quite understand, he didn't want to take Loretta into his room and suggested they use his car. When she asked what he wanted Francis told her that in the past three days he'd slept only a handful of hours, had given the heave-ho to yet another job, yet another attempt at normal life, abandoned the one woman he probably should've married, had come close to throwing himself from a waterfall, nearly died in a car accident, and may or may not have seen a car burn to its tyres on the interstate, this last being indicative of the various hallucinations, both visual and aural, plaguing him to the point he wasn't even sure if she – Loretta – existed.

'Oh, I exist all right. You'll learn that soon enough, sweetie.'

'Maybe if you could just use your hands. That's all.'

'That's all? That'll run you fifty bucks. You can do it yourself for nothing.'

Loretta unbuckled Francis's belt, opened his jeans. From her bag she took a sample-size tube of moisturizing lotion. She squeezed some into her palm and smoothed it on. Francis closed his eyes. He tried to empty his mind, focus on the rasping brush of sand against the car. Maybe this was the answer. Just this. But then she got him hard and started taking her time and Francis imagined it was Kathy beside him in the passenger seat touching him, moving her hand in slow, even strokes, her eyes on his. He had to keep from speaking her name, had to remind himself he was in Vegas, in his car in a motel parking lot in a sandstorm, paying for this. He reached to touch her. Opened his eyes. In the dark she looked like Kathy.

Control, he thought.

'Just lie still,' he heard Kathy's throaty, soothing voice. The touch of an Aussie lilt. 'Don't move.'

This is just a dream. It's not real.

'No worries.'

Francis imagined returning home, imagined Kathy waiting for him – though he would more than deserve it if she wasn't. '*Let's go,*' he'd say. And she'd say, '*It's about time.*' They'd take her boat, cruise down the coast to the

Caribbean. Take turns at the wheel. Make love on the deck. Sun, water, wind. He'd be glad to be off the land and all the shapes it offered, shapes that dictated the way you moved; be glad to be out of the isolated protection of his car and on the flat surface of the sea. He imagined fishing for dinner, sleeping when he was tired, watching the stars. The smell of salt. Imagined Kathy's giddy moans as she came. The lap of waves against the hull. Skimming the surface. In the state he was in it was possible for him to believe he was on her boat. That this car was her cabin. The noise of the street that of the ocean; the sand the whip of water off the crests of waves. They could spend the rest of their lives like that, moving from island to island – adrift. All he hoped was that she wouldn't ask any questions. Was it too much? He didn't see how he could've done it any other way. Everyone had their demons. He'd long ago learned from his bouts, his continual attempts at maintenance which he'd always hoped would help him make his way through the world, that rebirth was impossible. There was no way to ever completely wipe the slate clean.

Control. Stop.

'It doesn't matter,' he heard Kathy say, but he wasn't so sure. Not so sure at all.

As he came he had to remind himself again this was not Kathy. This was a hooker from Texas with bad make-up and fake boobs who went by the name of Loretta with him in his car in a motel parking lot in Las Vegas nowhere near the ocean.

She wiped her hands clean. From his wallet Francis took five twenties, handed the bills to Loretta who slipped them into her bag and got out, taking the used tissues with her.

Forgive us our trespasses, he thought after she shut the door. From the passenger seat he brushed away the sand that had swept in while the door was open. He laughed.

Hundred bucks on red, he thought.

Bust, he thought.

If You Came to Watch Me Die

[*For* Shane MacGowan]

Sober Up, was all the note read. His hands trembling, Sean picked up the letter from the table. The paper was plain, maybe even office paper. The writing unmistakably female. An elegant, simple slant. The tall *S* and *B*, the curve of her capitalized *U*, the loop at the bottom of the *P* – it was beautiful. But who would write such a thing? *Sober Up.* Jaysis. No signature, no return address. It wasn't his usual fan mail. He received hundreds of letters a year. Letters from women promising anything he wanted. Some would include pictures of themselves. Some would be of them naked, some with their legs spread open for him. Others would say, *I want to make you happy.* Or, *Let me love you.* Or once, *When I'm lonely I dream of you and I become happy because I know I'm not alone and that you are there with me and I'm there with you and together like this we can die.* Those from blokes were different. The Yanks they'd say something like, *You're the balls;* or, *Killer songs.* If they were Paddies or Jocks they might say, *Fuck the Brits.* Some of them quoted his own songs back to him. Most wanted to drink with him if he ever came to their city. But he'd never gotten anything like this. Not from a stranger.

'Fuckin' Jaysis. Sober up? What the fuck does she know? Sober up. Jaysis.'

Sean opened the room's liquor cabinet. These days even on a binge he tried to hold off on the drink until at least noon, or at the earliest eleven, but here he was wide awake at seven in the morning still half-drunk from last night's fun, shaking like a train. He had a show to do tonight – an Irish music festival up on Randall's Island. That was why he was here in New York. As good a place to be as any, at least the bars stayed open till four. Dawn, if you knew the right people. And now this letter. It was too much. But the liquor cabinet contained only rows of empty airplane bottles: Jack Daniels, Stolichnaya, Bacardi, José Cuervo, Tanquaray. He must've drunk them last night, then screwed the tops back on and put them back. What was he, fucking mad?

He got on the phone to room service. 'I need a bottle of something,' he whispered into the receiver. He didn't want to wake Eli asleep in the other bed. They'd been going out a couple of years now. She knew he was a drunk. She accepted the fact and tried only to keep him from killing himself, but she'd tear his head off if she knew he was hitting the piss this early in the morning.

'Excuse me,' said the person on the other end. 'Could you repeat what you said. I'm having a hard time understanding you.'

'A bottle. I need a bottle.'

'I'm sorry, you'll have to speak a little more clearly.'

'Fuckin' Yank, I said I need a fuckin' bottle. I need something to drink. Just get me something, I don't care what.'

'I'm sorry, I can't under—'

'A bottle,' he said again, louder.

He hung up the phone. He tried to remember Peter's room number, but couldn't. Peter was his manager. When he called the front desk they didn't have any easier time understanding him and he hung up again. He pulled on his shoes, remembered to grab his sunglasses, some cash. Fucking American money, it all looked alike. Every bill the same size and colour. What did they think you were, sober? Jaysis, they made it hard on you in this country.

In the lobby he felt sure they were all looking at him. Last night's clothes, stinking of alcohol. Smoking a fag in an obvious no smoking environment. Just another way the Americans wouldn't let you die. When a uniformed doorman asked him to extinguish his cigarette he dropped it on the carpet. Outside he tried to light another one, but the shakes were coming harder and he had a difficult time of it. Seeing this, another doorman snapped a zippo from his pocket and lit Sean's cigarette.

'You're a good man,' Sean said.

'Excuse me, sir.'

'A good man. Maybe you know where there's a bottle to be had.'

'I'm sorry, sir, it must be the accent. I can't understand what—'

'S'allright.' Sean wandered away down the street. He didn't want to say anything more. He liked black people. They reminded him of the Irish. A black woman, he was sure, would never write anything like *Sober Up*. Nor an Irish girl. Even a Brit – he could give them that much credit. The note had surely come from an American. He hadn't thought to look at the postage stamp, though. Fucking *Sober Up*. It sounded American, didn't it.

Normally he didn't fancy beer much, the way it bloated him and how much it took to get a buzz, but it was all he could find this early, so he bought a six pack of Budweiser and walked in the direction of where he thought he remembered an Irish pub to be. He'd been there loads of times, probably even last night. Even if they weren't open they'd recognize him and serve him up something hard. Halfway through the first can of foam, though, he had to stop to empty the contents of his stomach onto the sidewalk. For support he leaned against a building. The few people on the sidewalk this early on a Saturday morning ignored him. Or else they glanced at him, then ignored him. You had to love New York. A city where they let a man retch in peace.

As these things went, today was better than most days in his past. Days that had made him a bit of a legend when he'd still played with his old band. Once he'd collapsed at Heathrow airport the night before they were to open for Dylan in San Francisco. Ended up a week in hospital. Then their whole last tour he'd been too frail to make it through more than one or two songs a night, until they finally just got someone else to sing. That was before they'd kicked him out. His fucking band mates. For his own health, they'd said. Fuck, they hadn't thought he was going to live a minute longer, that's what – and by most accounts he probably should've died by now. But here he was, still performing, writing the best fucking songs of his life with a band willing to stay true to their roots and go wherever he'd take them. What was the old band doing now, eh? They were putting out albums full of shite. Maybe one or two decent songs, but mostly pure shite. Where was the poetry in it, that's what he wanted to know?

After he finished vomiting, Sean staggered to the kerb and waved down a cab.

'Paddy Reiley's. Twenty something and something.'

The driver couldn't understand him either. Finally Sean managed to make it clear where he wanted to go, but neither he nor the driver knew the address and they ended up criss-crossing all the streets in the Twenties for an hour trying to find it. In the meantime Sean finished his six pack. He had the taxi stop so he could vomit again and by chance recognized the place he was looking for.

'Drunkard's luck,' he said, handing the cabby a crumpled handful of bills.

The door was open, the inside dark. Already two men sat at the bar, each with a glass of whiskey and a pint of Guinness. Sean smiled. He wouldn't be alone. And there he was, a barman he recognized. Someone he knew could understand what he said. Or would at least pretend to. He sat down. He pointed at the empty space on the bar in front of him. On the walls there hung posters of Irish bands. Van Morrison, The Chieftains, The Dubliners, Christy Moore. Others. There were posters of Sean's old band, pictures of the eight of them taken at this very bar. A promotional poster of Sean's solo album, *An Ugly Way to Live*. Sean McCallister, it read, and below an overblown close-up of his face, broken teeth and all. He wasn't a rich bloke, but he made enough money to fix his teeth if he wanted. He was proud of them, though, and besides, there were better things to spend money on.

'How's it then?' the barman asked as he put down a large glass of Martini. Vermouth was Sean's effort at cutting back.

'Fuckin' Yanks, can't understand a word you say.'

'Are you after playing the Fleahd tonight?'

Sean shrugged. 'Maybe I'll just spend me entire fuckin' day here. Wha?'

'You won't want to be doing that?'

Sean threw back half the glass of whiskey. It burned. In a moment he felt better. The shakes began to disappear. Another half-glass and the world would be in order again. He'd be happy for a little while. It was then, when you were happy like that, it didn't matter how you'd feel later, in the morning. It didn't matter how crabby you'd get. Didn't matter about the vomiting and the shaking. The paranoia. The occasional delirium visions. When you were happy like that. That's what people who weren't drunks didn't understand. That for a time you could actually see God. You could. But like with everything, you had to pay. God didn't give his grace freely.

When he finished with the glass Sean signalled for another.

'You're Sean McCallister, aren't ya?' one of the men at the other end of the bar asked in a Tipperary accent, Sean's birthplace. He was older than Sean, almost his da's age, but not so old as he looked. He had the drinker's stance.

'I am.'

'Let me stand you one.'

'Your man here's got to perform tonight,' the barman said even as he set down Sean's second full glass.

'Ach, what's a glass? He'll play if he feckin' wants to. That's your man Sean McCallister there. That's the way he's been and that's the way he'll be. Now I'd like to stand him a round if he'll have it.'

The barman shrugged. He lined up a shot of whiskey for Sean and one for the man. The ginger lady.

'*Slainte*,' Sean said, raising his.

'*Slainte*.'

They drank.

'Yiz ever be talking to any of your old mates, then?' the man asked Sean.

'Wha? Nah. Paddy and Michael, sure. See 'em at the Whiskey in London now and then. None of the others. I don't want anything to do with 'em.'

'I heard ya'd gone sober. They said Eli moved yiz off to Dublin to get you away from the drink.' It wasn't an accusation.

'She did.' Sean smiled. Only another drunk could get away with saying something like that. Only a drunk could point out that another drunk wasn't off the booze without the hint of judgment, just the understanding that it hadn't happened. A drunk wouldn't have to ask why. 'I tried to stick to the beer, you know, but the foam makes me stomach hurt.'

The man nodded. 'I liked your album,' he said. 'The best since *Grace*. Feckin' brilliant.'

Grace was the third album from when he'd still been with the band, and following on the success of their second, *I Am Going*, had broken them through on the British charts and even given them a hit single. Those two had been their first to go gold and had started their cult following here in the States. But that was ten years and a couple of lifetimes ago.

'You're still writing, then?' the man asked.

'I am. Thinking of one right now. About this letter I got. All it said was "sober up". Can you fuckin' believe that? Some bleedin' American bird telling me "sober up"? It's a fucking laugh, is what it is.'

'Maybe she knows. Maybe ya should listen.'

'Ah, fuck you. Not you too.'

'Maybe ya should.'

Like that, they drank.

Sean made it back to the hotel by five. He hadn't had enough money to pay for his drinks but the bartender had waved him off, told him it was on the house, just to make sure he put on a good show tonight. 'Don't be an ejit,' he'd said as he put Sean into a taxi.

'Do what ya want, Sean,' the other man had said.

Sean handed the taxi driver what was left of his money. He didn't know if it was enough. He'd find out shortly if it wasn't, he was sure.

In the lobby he found Eli waiting in a seat. 'Where the fuck have you been?'

'Ah, you're a sight, aren't you?'

'Fuck off and answer my question. You've been on the piss, haven't you? Before I even woke you were to the bar, is that it? Jaysis, I've a mind to smack the rest of your teeth out.'

This was why he loved her. His last girlfriends had always begged and pleaded for him to stop, to promise not to do it again. With Eli he was just like a child. He went to put his arms around her. After a moment she gave in. She said, 'You worry me, Sean. I don't want you dying on me.'

'With you to love me I can never die.'

'You're full of shite, Sean.'

'I promise you I'll never die.'

'I don't want your promises.'

Sean wanted only to curl up, lay his head on Eli's lap and be held. He didn't know what he could give in return. Except his love. But he would give everything there was of him for the assurance she would never leave.

Upstairs in the room they kissed and tried to make love but it was useless and Sean passed out. He awoke to Eli kneeling naked beside him sponging his body. She looked at his face while she did so. She didn't smile.

'What time is it? Wha?' He felt groggy, not sure where he was. His head hurt.

'You have time, don't worry yourself.'

'I can't miss me show.'

'You won't.'

'They don't think I'll be there.'

'I know.'

Eli ran the sponge lightly between his thighs.

'Ah, luv, you're valiant—'

'Shh.' Eli put her finger to his lips. She continued with her sponging.

'I love you,' Sean said.

'I know.'

Most of his band had spent the day in the city or drinking or at the festival watching the other acts. At seven Eli, Peter, and Sean left the hotel in a limo. Sean smoked a cigarette and sipped from a glass of vodka. It was like taking medicine. Eli drank wine; Peter a can of pub draught.

'Did I tell you?' he said. 'I got a letter. From a woman.'

'Oh, Jaysis, do I have to hear this?' Eli said. 'I don't want to know what other women want to do to you.'

'Nah, this isn't like that. This woman, she must be a Yank, all she wrote was "sober up". That's all. Nothing signed. Can you fuckin' believe it?'

Peter and Eli were quiet.

Sean said, 'What the fuck is she doing sending me a note like that? She doesn't know me, does she? She doesn't know shite.'

'Maybe she does,' Eli said.

'What are you saying, then?'

'I'm saying maybe she does know you.'

'Ah, Jesus, Sean,' Peter said. 'It's only a letter. You get them all the time. What's it matter if this bird is telling you to sober up. I've been telling you the same for years. So has Eli.'

'Ah, fuck you.'

'And there you go.'

'You're a right bastard is what you are. A right fuckin' cunt.'

'I'm not preaching to you, but sooner or later it's going to kill you. That's what happens to drinkers. Either they sober up or they drink themselves to death. Look at your man Brendan Behan.'

'Well, then I guess I'm going to die.' Sean smiled, showing his broken teeth. They didn't believe him, but he had no intention of dying. Once, sure, back in the days when he couldn't do one song without a lyric sheet, one set without puking on stage, when he'd collapsed on any number of occasions while still holding onto the mike.

The crowd would roar. Episodes like that had only served to make him more of a legend. But not any more. He didn't care about the fame, the notoriety. They could have it. What no one seemed to grasp was that he was holding on tighter now than he ever had in the past. Just barely holding on, but holding on none the less. He had no intention of letting go.

By the time they arrived at Randall's Island their stage had been set, the sound check completed. The band waited backstage. He heard someone say there were well over thirty thousand people at the festival. Most were gathered at the main stage where Van Morrison was headlining. Sean and his band topped the bill on one of the smaller stages while on the other a popular young Scottish fiddler would be performing. All at the same time. In front of Sean's stage, though, a crowd of three thousand already waited and he could hear his name being chanted. Sean, Sean, Sean, Sean: a sound like the ocean.

Sean looked at the set list. Most of it the audience wouldn't recognize; it was mostly new songs, some old. Fuck it. He liked the new bits best. Sitting at that bar this afternoon he'd even begun to write another.

'How's about this?' he asked his band. Imagining tin whistle, accordion, electric guitar, banjo all working through a punked-up reel, Sean gave them what he'd come up with:

> Sober up, she said to me, but how was I to know
> She'd take from me everything I had,
> My blood, my love, my dough.

Eyes as bright as diamonds, hair like soft spun gold,
She'd a smile that could kill a child
And a heart of burning cold.

I met her in a bar, now she's left me in the dirt.
A goddess, she was beautiful
It made my eyeballs hurt.
In pubs and bars and railroad cars she'd whisper in me ear,
Come with me, now, little boy,
What have ye to fear?

I followed her around the world, I chased her through
    damnation.
I begged her for all that she had stolen
But all she offered was salvation.
The night long gone in a club downtown thinking what she
    said,
Love me now and till the end of time,
Love me till you're dead.

Call me a dog
Call me a hound
I was lost
But now I'm found.

He repeated the last verse, then stopped, shy suddenly.
They seemed to like it. They were nodding their heads,
tapping out a rhythm. Finn suggested just a little tweak.
Brian thought it was fine. Terry said they could fit it to this
wild reel they'd been working on. They gave him bits of it.

Sean mumbled some of the words, letting them fall on top as if into allocated places.

'We could do it tonight, even,' someone said. 'What do you think, Sean? We could do it.'

Sean couldn't say what he thought. He felt high with excitement. An excitement that came with something new, with something working out. It left him frightened. A song, anything coming together – he thought of all the thousands of ways it could have failed, come apart in the process. Never existed. How tender such a thing, how fragile. Pure luck, that's what it was. Pure brilliant luck. It left him humble in ways he couldn't tell his band, or anyone.

'Yeah, sure.' He shrugged. When he reached for a bottle of vodka on the small bar set up in the dressing room his hand shook so hard he knocked it to the floor where it smashed. The band didn't seem to notice. Eli and Peter watched him. Eli inched forward. Sean looked at his hand. Didn't they know he was shaking with excitement. 'What the fuck,' he said. 'We'll do it last.'

'You want me to write the words down for you?' Peter asked.

'Ah, fuck, no. I just wrote them this afternoon. Got them here on me hand.' Sean held up the back of his hand, but they were gone. Eli must have accidentally sponged them away in his sleep. 'No matter. I remembered them once already.'

'If you're sure.'

'Yeah, I'm sure. Fuckin' Jaysis.' This time he went for the gin and got it around the neck.

Sean took care not to fall on his way across the stage. It felt

like a lifetime with three or four thousand faces following
him. He spoke into the mike, indicated with his thumb for
the volume to be turned higher. The band started, tight and
fast. He gripped the mike with both hands and began
spitting out a song in his trademark laconic slur. The words
came, falling into place. Occasionally he moved them one
way or another with his voice. Up or down as the song
demanded. He hit every note, like he always did these days.
In between verses he sipped from his cup of gin, took drags
off his cigarette. The sound wasn't quite right. He stalked to
the sound booth at the side of the stage. 'What the fuck?' he
shouted. 'How's about some fucking volume on me mike. I
can't even hear meself.' Before the song came around to the
next verse he was back at centre stage. He finished the song.
The crowd cheered, called out his name.

'Good fuckin' evening. Now here's another one.'

One after another he followed the prompt of the music.
As long as the band played he was there.

Three quarters of the way through the set Peter came on
stage. 'You have to go. Instrumental.'

'Wha? Yeah, sure.'

He wanted to keep singing, but staggered off, Peter's
hand touching his elbow. Backstage he made himself vomit,
then smoked another cigarette.

'It's going all right,' Peter said. 'You're doing great, Sean.
Are you holding up?'

'What am I, a fucking boxer? Jaysis.'

'He's just making sure you're all right,' Eli said. 'You
don't look well. You've gone pale as a sheet. And you're
shaking like the bejesus. Can you even stand out there?'

'Am I singing me songs?'

'Yeah—'

'Well, then I'm bloody fine.'

When the instrumental was over he went back on stage. He waited while the band readied itself. He wasn't sure what he was waiting for, but he needed the music to sing. Suddenly Peter appeared and slipped a cigarette between his fingers. He took a drag. To the audience it might look like he was just a shaky mannequin fed on alcohol and tobacco. Could be that's what Peter and Eli thought. Could be they were scared. His band, though, they had faith in him. They understood that he fed himself. He was alive inside. It was enough.

When it came to the last song he said, 'This is for whoever sent me that note. The one that said "sober up".' He took a drag of his cigarette. It looked like he might say more, but then the band started in. The reel was new to him and he missed the first place to come in. He had to wait what seemed like an eternity for it to come around again. He hoped he wouldn't forget the words. He was having some trouble seeing. Then the old fears: that at any moment his legs would give way beneath him and he'd collapse. His band was probably thinking the same. Eli. Peter. The audience, they were waiting for it to happen. Fucking vultures. They were waiting to eat him up, have a go at his bloody entrails.

He heard the reel come around again, leaned his face into the mike, but then let it pass. It hadn't felt right. He walked to the sound man. He felt top heavy.

'More accordion,' he said.

'Are you all right?'

'More fucking accordion. This is Irish music.'

'Sean, you all right?' Peter asked. 'You don't look good, mate. Why don't we go now? I don't want you doing too much. It's not worth it. You've been drinking hard all day.'

Sean ignored Peter and walked back to his mike.

'Sorry, boys and girls, but if you came to watch me die it's not gonna happen.' They probably couldn't understand him. Fuck it. The song came around and this time he came in. Missed a couple of words, an entire line. The last verse he sang as a chorus, repeating it twice, then at the end again. It felt rough. The song wasn't quite on. When it was over he said, 'Again,' and they started from the top. This time they nailed it, even down to the finish.

Sean didn't want to leave the stage. He felt like he could go on all night, one song after another. The band was looking at him, waiting for the sign. They would go with him. They wouldn't let him die. But then Peter was beside him, ushering him off the stage. He could hear the roar of the crowd, his name being called.

Backstage Eli took a hold of him. 'Jaysis, you're a mess. I'm taking you home.'

Sean didn't say anything. He knew they were wrong, Eli and Peter. Tonight wouldn't have been the night. Maybe another night, but not tonight. He wouldn't have died tonight. He was sure of that. Eli had her arm around him to make sure he didn't fall or smash into anything. He let her.

In the back seat of the car taking them back to Manhattan Eli said, 'You won't stop, will you, Sean? This business is killing you.'

He wasn't sure what she was talking about, so he said, 'No.'

'I love you, Sean,' Eli said, crying.

Sean put his arm around her. She felt cold. He wanted to warm her, and with both arms held her to him. There were times, Sean thought, you were so happy it didn't matter what came after. A happiness so deep and twisted it could make you cry.

'Did I tell you?' he said. 'I got this letter. All it said was "sober up".'

Part Four
IN A FURIOUS INSTANT

Down in Miami Forty Years Ago

There is something. Forty years ago when I was eighteen down in Miami, I killed a man. Louis Baxter. He was a member of the city's first coloured police force, though as they were only patrolmen and coloured their authority was limited to the Negro neighbourhood in which I grew up, which accounts for the fact the white officers made no genuine fuss over his killing and never pursued any investigation.

Baxter used to find me on the streets of our neighbourhood at night when I was alone. He'd lead me into an alley and lay in on me with his billy club – on my neck and spine and kidneys so as not to leave any scars or bruises, calling me a no-good nigger like he didn't know he was one himself. I'd try to stand up to his blows, but I was just eighteen and skinny and he had me on size. I went down. There'd be blood in my mouth and from my nose and my pants they'd be wet with piss. He wouldn't stop. He would go on until I cried, then tell me to stand and go at me again. My face wet with tears, I'd curse him for a nigger, swearing he'd die, he would, that I'd kill him. And so I got myself a gun and I shot him.

*

Forty years later a detective, a white guy looking like he doesn't know why he is where he is, carrying his body like dead weight, comes to my apartment in Morningside Heights. He says his name is Harrison and he wants to ask me some questions. So I say, 'Sure.'

He asks if I am Nelson Stiles and I tell him, 'I am.'

Do I recognize the name Louis Baxter? he asks me and I say, 'Yes, I do.'

He asks if I killed Baxter, back forty years ago down in Miami. There was a witness, he says, saw me shoot him. Says she's come speak out after all these years of silence.

'And why, if I may inquire, is she speaking now?' I ask.

'Guess she was scared. Thought the man who did Baxter might do her.' Harrison shrugs. 'She's old, close to eighty; could be she's thinking she's going to die soon and wants to clear her conscience. Could be she's afraid of going to Hell.' Harrison pulls a book from the shelf he's leaning against and flips through the pages. 'You afraid of going to Hell, Stiles?'

' 'Course I am. But it wasn't me who killed him,' I say. For though I am an honest man, this lie comes easily to me. 'I'm a good Christian and I've been a good citizen. I've done as good as I could, what with being a black man from the South.'

As I speak I take the bag I was packing from the bedroom.

'Going away?' Harrison asks.

I tell him I'm to visit my daughter, Clarice. 'She's at Harvard getting her PhD in Public Health. I go every month to see her.'

Harrison sits. He says he's sorry to have bothered me and

doesn't want me to miss my bus, but their witness is Mrs Wilson, she lived just around the corner from my family down in Miami. She swears it was me she saw shoot Louis Baxter. And Dade County's investigation shows I left Miami the day after his killing.

'Well, I can tell you I didn't kill Louis Baxter, Detective.'

Harrison stands again. 'You like to read a lot?' he asks. He nods at my bookcase.

I tell him I've tried to educate myself.

'These are some pretty serious books.' He points them out: Aristotle; Plato; Kant's *The Critique of Pure Reason*; Sartre; Thomas Aquinas. 'This is serious stuff. Must be difficult to get through.' Harrison leafs through *The Confessions of St Augustine*, stopping to glance at the dog-eared pages. It's the only one of them I've ever finished. 'You're a God-fearing man, Stiles, what about the Bible? You read the Bible?'

'I've read the Good Book.'

'Go to church?'

'I'm a good Christian, I already told you that.'

Harrison replaces the book. 'It's a shame about Baxter. If he'd been a white officer Dade would've nailed the man who killed him; they wouldn't have let it go so long. Probably would've gotten the chair, too.'

'Well, I'm much impressed to see the concern for the life of a black man some forty years later, but I'm not so sure it's a shame he wasn't white. You can't bring back someone's life by taking that of another. God doesn't even things up that way.'

'Be that as it may, Mr Stiles, but there are laws in this

country we need to abide by. There is a moral standard. I'm sure with all your reading you can appreciate that.'

After seeing Harrison out I sit in my chair, my palms soft with sweat. My travel bag is open on the footstool. For a long moment there I don't look at anything.

It's funny, how in the same instant the life of another can be the most precious thing in the world and in the next . . . Nothing. Just like that. One shot, through his chest. Dead. I still have the picture in my mind – Baxter lying on the ground, his shirt soaked with blood, a puddle spreading beneath him and leaking out from under his sides. He was dead, for sure, or dying, but he was twitching, so I shot him again, from closer. And it's this second shot I hear. Not in my head, but like a real shot, right up next to and in my ear. A ringing sound. And the smell of burned powder – a sharp smell that gets inside you and stays there.

I'd forgotten. No – I'd stopped remembering, so that I can say to the detective with a straight face, *No, I didn't kill Louis Baxter.*

Mary, my beloved wife, died of cancer thirty-one years ago. It started in her breasts, but by the time we learned of it it'd already spread to her lymph nodes. There was nothing we could do and for three months I watched her die. I figured it was some kind of punishment from God, a penance for the life I'd taken from Louis Baxter, and the whole time she lay dying I prayed to God not to take her, to take me instead, praying like I hadn't prayed since I was a little boy afraid of the dark begging for morning to bring light to my room. Before she died I tried to explain about Baxter, explain how sorry I was she had to die for me this way, but Mary she didn't know what I was saying any more. I was crying and begged again for God to take me, but I knew even as I did that he wouldn't ever, no matter how much I begged and prayed. Things just don't even up that way.

At the Mass for Mary's funeral I was scared to step inside the church on account of what God might think of my impunity, setting foot in his sanctuary. I had no right being there. And all the congregation, I figured, knew and were wondering how I dared come before the altar of God if I didn't do so on my knees. I haven't been in a church since, though what I said to Harrison is true, I believe in God. I believe in his laws.

Now, thirty-one years after Mary's death, I take the Bible from the drawer where I keep it and hold it in my hands and feel its weight. I don't open it. Usually the Book gives me solace. It reassures me I am indeed in the hands of someone who can forgive me, but not this day. Instead a dreadful, inevitable feeling takes hold of me and I put down the Book and leave my apartment.

On the street I head for the precinct house where Harrison said I could find him. My hands and arms and feet are cold. At the same time I'm sweating a hot sweat. I can feel my heart in my body. A feeling like when I watched Mary die, when the cancer finally broke her and her chest stopped its painful rise and fall and her own heart quieted. I cried and what I felt then was sorrow; and at the same time relief that it was over. It was later, when I tried to sleep that night, the most awful thought struck me, a thought that makes me shudder still to think of it, that it was Mary who died, not me. That I'd somehow cheated death. The death I'd wanted. That I'd cheated God. That it was me who was alive, who'd not been granted life, but had stolen it.

At the precinct I have to wait to see Harrison. Across from me in the lobby three black kids sit with their hands cuffed behind their backs, talking and laughing and cursing. 'Hey black man,' they keep saying, but I don't answer. They ask me if I'm mute. Deaf. 'Maybe he just plain dumb,' one of them says.

A clock hangs on the wall above their heads. There's time still for me to catch the next bus and be in Boston by ten. I could tell Clarice something, it wouldn't matter what, except her partner she's been living with for two years, Tanya, a white woman and easily the meanest, angriest bitch I've ever had cause to meet, would probably make a comment.

It's a shame about that, really, on account I wouldn't mind having a grandson to be grandpa to. I've always imagined myself telling the boy about the way it used to be down south. Black neighbourhoods; black schools; blacks-only water fountains and blacks-only toilets. And he, he'd never have to see a *Whites Only* sign. But that's the way it was. We had our own nigger cops and no one cared what we did to each other. Sometimes I'll say to Clarice, 'Can't you get yourself artificially inseminated, just for your papa? Just so I have someone to leave my name to.' Tanya, she'll give me a look like I'm some kind of bastard out to keep my daughter down, but Clarice knows I'm just fooling and she'll say, camping it up like she's on a TV sit-com or something, she'll say that if she ain't gonna let no man put his penis in there she sure as hell ain't gonna let no doctor put no man's sperm in there.

When Harrison finally comes out he doesn't seem to recognize me. I tell him who I am, tell him I lied to him; it was me who killed Baxter down in Miami. It was me who shot him.

Behind me the black kids can't stop their laughing. Harrison looks over at them, then says he'll have to arrest me and get an official confession. He takes me through a door and to a desk where he has me sign a paper explaining my rights. When I'm done I have to wait while Harrison finds a room for my confession.

In the room there are an aluminium table and two chairs. A video camera is set up facing one of the chairs. Harrison brings us each a cup of coffee, then motions for me to sit. 'Just ignore the camera,' he says. 'Just tell it to me the way it happened, Nelson.' He takes a moment to adjust something on the camera, then asks me to state my name, my residence, my age. Finally he asks, 'Did you kill Louis Baxter?'

'I did', I say.

'And did you have any reason for this?'

I don't say anything at first. I don't want to, on account of the way it sounds to me after all this time. When it all happened I was a different person. Just a kid, eighteen. Thought I had the world licked. 'Well, sir,' I say, 'he used to beat me.'

'Beat you?'

I nod.

'Beat you, how?'

I tell Harrison how Baxter thought he was the shit that didn't stink, being a patrolman in a black neighbourhood and all. How he was a cocky bastard and I'd say things to him.

'What sort of things?'

'I'd tell him he wasn't no cop, just the white man's billy club, their nigger bully. It was on account of this Baxter beat me. It's nothing I'm proud of.' But the words, I don't feel right with them, they aren't the proper ones and feel all strange inside me, not like I'm lying, but like I don't want them attributed to me. Like that was someone else back then. What I want is to be honest and true to the facts, but what those facts are I can't be sure any more and I feel like I'm leaving something out, something vital that's been lost with time, dulled by these years of my daily life, and I don't feel at all certain the way I'm telling it is the way it really was.

'Baxter,' I say, 'he beat me because he could, because he had the badge to back him up. He used to say I had a mouth on me and that I was too smart for my own good and needed to learn some respect.' Harrison smokes a cigarette and listens as I try to explain I had no choice about taking the beatings. 'The white folks, they didn't give a damn what went down between us Negroes. As far as they were concerned the niggers could just as well kill themselves. And no way I could tell anyone in the neighbourhood; they'd have said I didn't have the balls to fight back. So I got myself a gun from a friend and the next time when Baxter came looking for me with that big, ugly grin on his face, I shot him.'

When we're through and there's nothing more for me to say

and Harrison has turned off the video camera, I ask if I can call Clarice. She answers and asks if anything is wrong; I'm supposed to be on the bus up to Boston. I tell her I won't be able to make it.

'Has something happened?'

'Clarice, now,' I say, 'there's something I have to tell you. Please just listen. I killed a man. I mean, forty years ago, back when I was growing up in Miami, I killed a man. A cop. A black cop. It was a long time ago, and I know that doesn't excuse it and I've done turned myself in. They've arrested me. But everything is going to be fine, you hear. I'm all right. You hear, Clarice? I'm still your father. Still the man who raised you.'

There is a pause, like Clarice has gone away for a moment, then she asks, 'What will happen to you?' The way she is talking, it's like she hasn't heard a word I've said. 'Is there a statute of limitations? What about some sort of plea bargain? Do you have a lawyer? Do you want me to come down?'

'No, no, baby. You stay where you are. Everything will be OK.'

'I'm coming down.'

'Now, baby,' I start, but she says please not to call her baby.

Lowering my voice to a whisper, I say, 'I don't want you to think I'm some kind of murderer. All right, Clarice? I don't want you thinking that. Not in my heart.'

'I know you're not.'

'And this, it's something your mother never knew about, OK. OK?'

Clarice sighs. 'I'm not sure how I'm supposed to react.'

'I don't know.' I tighten my grip on the phone.

'I'm with you, Dad, no matter what, you know that. People do crazy things, doesn't make them crazy – but I just—'

'I'm not crazy, baby.'

'Will you tell me what happened?' Clarice asks.

But I can't say anything. I don't feel right explaining to my daughter what happened down in Miami. I can't justify to her about killing Baxter the way I did to the camera, the way I've been doing to myself, because there are no justifications, just actions. All I can do is tell Clarice I have to get going, because I can't face her, the image of Mary.

There is a moment of silence and I wait for the right words to drop from Heaven, but there aren't any words and I say goodbye.

Once I'm off the phone a clerk hands me into the custody of another officer who'll escort me to the central cell block. Before he leads me away Harrison takes my arm and pulls me aside. He says he's talked to Dade County and I'll be tried up here. I'll probably be getting a hearing in a couple of days. 'But Nelson,' he says, 'Dade was talking the death penalty.'

At the central cell block they put me in a cell with a black kid not past twenty who claims to have killed two people and shot up a whole lot more – gang-banging, he says – but the cops they don't got him on that. They got him on one count Grand Theft Auto and one count Aggravated Assault for jacking a Beemer from some white-ass yuppie. Says he'll be on the street again before I know it, though, 'cause he's got information the cops want. He ain't going to jail for stealing no motherfucking white man's car. Not without taking the motherfucker out.

It's then it hits me that Harrison is saving my life.

In the days before my hearing Harrison comes to see me. He says Clarice got a hold of him and she'll be coming down. He says she seems like a strong woman. And he's impressed by her achievements: started at City College, a scholarship to Yale, on to Harvard. 'You must be proud,' he says.

'She's done pretty good for a black woman.'

Harrison smokes half of a cigarette before he says anything. 'This is a strange case, Stiles. Strangest I've seen in twelve years as a detective. I don't know where to stand on this.' Harrison has this way of not looking at anything when he talks, like he's embarrassed, like it's some kind of weakness. 'I mean, you killed a man. I got the law on my side. And there's precedent. The guy was a cop, after all, even if he was just a—'

'Just a nigger?'

'Just a patrolman,' Harrison finishes.

He paces the cell. 'Could be you're being too hard on yourself. Could be you did the right thing, killing Baxter; maybe Baxter deserved it. God knows I've felt that way plenty of times. Like him.' He waves in the direction of my cell-mate. 'Right and wrong are tenuous things. Why not just shoot the asshole, get it over with?' The boy flashes his eyes at this. 'But then, you've got a good heart inside you, Stiles. That's the difference, isn't it?'

'It doesn't feel so good.'

'Well, that's what makes it what it is. That's what makes your heart what it is.'

The same afternoon I meet with my state-appointed lawyer. We sit on either end of a booth with a plexiglas divider between us. Through the intercom he tells me there's no way I'll go free on this one, even if the DA cuts a deal. Not for killing a cop, no matter how long ago. Not even with a confession. 'It's just not going to happen. But we have a good shot at leniency on account of the video-taped confession and your clean record. Especially if you talk that way to the judge. Stick to the stuff about how Baxter beat you. Be just the way you were and we're looking all right. Don't lose sight of that. But don't go thinking you're going to be set free, because it ain't gonna happen.'

The next day Clarice comes to see me. It's a meeting for which I am nervous to the point of shivering. This is not any way I ever imagined my daughter would see me.

We meet in the same room as I met my lawyer, in a booth just like that one. Next to us are other booths and other inmates talking to visitors. As she sits across from me she begins to cry. It's enough to break my heart then and there, though my heart, I've learned, is already a fragile thing.

'Please look at me,' Clarice says through her tears. I lift my head. 'Will you tell me what happened?'

'Clarice, baby,' I say. This isn't something I want for her to know, not ever. No daughter should have to know this about her father. 'I don't—'

'Daddy, please. You have to do this for me.' She lowers her voice. 'Daddy, please just tell me what happened.'

But whatever I say, it feels a lie, a spin on the truth, a

deflection. So I say, 'I killed a man, that's what happened, baby. It's as simple as that.'

'If he did something to you, Dad. Harrison didn't tell me anything but he made it sound like it was self-defence. Was it? A man has to defend himself. Haven't you always said that?'

'A man has to stand up for himself, but that's something else.' I look away from her, ashamed. What can I say? *That I was scared. That I hated him. That he hurt me.* These things don't seem so important any more and the truth, it feels, lies between them all.

'Dad, I want to be on your side. I am on your side, but you have to tell me, so I know the truth.'

'There are no sides.'

'But you had your reasons. Maybe they don't make what you did right, but maybe what you didn't wasn't wrong either. If you'd just tell—'

'The law is the law. It's all I'm left with.'

Clarice straightens her spine. I've pushed her away and I feel her close herself, shut her emotions off, and I wish I could say more, I do, explain to her that I killed a man out of malice and that I can't tell any more the difference between right and wrong, that everything I've done for her has been by way of penance, that my love for her is a means of redemption, but the words they aren't there, only my daughter, sitting straight-backed and resolute, looking at me through the plexiglas barrier, and I understand the sin I am guilty of is the lie of omission.

The morning after I shot Baxter I left Miami for New York, just the way Harrison has it down. Once there I got myself a cheap room and for a week all I did was lie in my bed with my blankets wrapped tight around me, trying to hide inside those blankets like when I was a kid and afraid of the dark. The whole time my thoughts they were going round and round my head, dwelling on what I'd done, but after a week I was out of money and I hadn't been eating a whole lot, so I got myself a job hauling cement sacks. Hard work, I hoped, would do me good.

I got an apartment and eventually the job pulling pallets at the warehouse where I'm still at. It was good work, working with my hands, and when they made me foreman I told them I preferred being on the floor. I was drinking a lot, from straight after my shift until I fell asleep. And I was gambling. I never had enough money for the really good life, but there was always enough to go out with the boys: shoot pool, meet girls – all the things you do to keep yourself busy and your mind cloudy, except that you can't get away from the things you've done. All you can do is stop remembering, just tuck that knowledge away in some corner of your soul where you never have to look at it or touch it. But it's there and you can't ever get rid of it, not even when you die, because that knowledge is a part of you and will always come along with you.

Christmas six years later I returned to Miami to see my family. The bus ride took thirty-three hours and the whole time I didn't sleep a wink until I got to where I was having these waking dreams about cops waiting for me or hauling the bus to the side of the road. Every time we stopped at a station I sank in my seat to hide, sure at any moment they'd be stepping onto the bus. When I got to Miami, though, no one seemed to care or remember. Not a word, no trace. I was free. It was an easy enough thing to believe in the sunshine they got down there. Though as a black man and as a human I can say you are never free.

It was on this trip I met Mary and when I left I took her with me. I warned her about the weather in New York, but she said that no Yankee weather could keep her from the man she loved. And looking into her eyes, feeling her small arms around me, hearing her comforting whispers in the dark: how easy it was to forget. How easy and how pleasant. A year later Clarice was born. Between the two of them, Clarice and Mary, they were the best thing that ever happened to this man's life. Turned it right around. I stopped most my drinking and all my gambling and stayed home. I figured I was finally making good. Then, three years after Clarice was born, just when Mary and I were thinking about having another baby, maybe try for a boy this time, Mary got sick with the cancer. Three months later she was dead.

Things were rough for me. I had a daughter to raise and without the pay Mary'd been drawing working part-time for a jeweller money was tight, but I managed. I cut out my drinking altogether and never saw the boys any more, except when I could take little Clarice along. They adored her and understood, but when she wasn't around they all said I should find her a mother. Mary would understand. 'Course no one knew about what had happened in Miami. No one.

When Clarice started school things got easier. I didn't need a baby-sitter any more except once in a while when I went out. It was around then I started reading – first Augustine, then Aquinas – but like I said, I couldn't get myself through them. I tried to meet some ladies and now and then I got to know one and like her, and Clarice, the way a little girl will, she'd ask, 'Will she be my mommy?' But these relationships never lasted, failing on account of being alone with the memory of Mary was more satisfying to me. One woman, she said I was afraid to love, to live again. I let her believe that even as she shut the door on me.

My friends all said I was just plain crazy.

In high school Clarice aced nearly every course she took. By the time she got to City College she was recommending books for me to read. The heavier ones: Kant; Sartre; Descartes. She said it was great to see me want to educate myself, except I never got to reading any of those on account of the language and not believing what they had to offer. When Clarice was at Yale I asked her if she had any boyfriends. It was all right for me to be alone, but I was worried about her. I was also thinking about a grandson.

At her graduation she introduced me to Tanya. She said they were moving in together in Boston. I don't know what bothered me more as I reached to shake the hand Tanya offered, Clarice being a lesbian or her partner being white?

At the arraignment I plead guilty to murder in the second degree on account of a self-defence plea even though it carries the same time as Murder One: twenty-five to life. My lawyer asks for bail to be set, but the DA argues there is never any bail in the case of a police officer being murdered no matter how long ago and the judge agrees. The trial is set for a date nine months away.

Clarice, alone on the bench behind me, sits in the likeness of her mother: stalwart, knowing her lot is to accept these events as they come. Her face is drawn, like she hasn't slept in days; like the one thing in the world she wants to do is sit down and stop everything: the turning of the earth; the passage of time; all movement. Stop – without a thought in her head. Without the knowledge that her father killed a man and is going to jail, perhaps for the rest of his life. Despite this, she manages to give me a smile as I'm escorted from the courtroom, my head down, my hands cuffed in front of me.

Along with a few other detainees I'm taken to a penitentiary upstate where I'm given a cell to myself. It's a simple thing: three walls, a bed, a desk, toilet, the barred gate. My only possessions are some books. On her first visit Clarice brings me photos of her and of Mary she's taken from my apartment. She hopes it will make me feel at least a little bit at home and it breaks my heart again to see her efforts at accepting these events as normal. She also brings me some books and a diary bound in leather: 'Just to jot things down in.' Though I know I'll never write in it.

She asks how I'm doing, if I'm all right.

'I'm fine.'

'Are you eating all right?'

'Yeah.'

'Are you in any danger?'

'I'm fine.'

Clarice looks like she's about to say something, show anger at my curt, closed responses, but she doesn't allow herself that and abruptly stands and turns away and heads for the door out of the visiting room. Before the door closes on her I see the slight heave of her shoulders like she's crying and I want to go after her, but even if I tried to speak she wouldn't hear me through the plexiglas.

There are other visits, each more strained than the first, and I wonder why she comes at all and why I still, no matter how much I fear the silence, look forward to seeing her. The thing is, we just don't have anything to say. I ask her about her research and about Boston and even ask about Tanya. She says these things are too trivial to be talking about. What she wants is to talk about me, how I'm doing, but I don't want to tell her anything – not about the details of my imprisonment; about what happened down in Miami; about Mary. What is there to say? It's enough for Clarice to see me like this, I don't want to expose to her the quiet fear growing inside me that my life, who I am, will be judged solely in the context of Baxter's murder.

I have a routine. I shower, have breakfast, then try to read some of the books Clarice brings me. A page here and there before I close the covers and shut my eyes. For exercise I walk circles in the yard. To walk off my thoughts. At lunch I listen to the other inmates, then there's another turn in the yard, then dinner. In the evenings I write letters until I'm tired enough to sleep. Most of the letters I never send. They're long and apologetic, telling Clarice all the things I'm not able to speak about in person, sprung from the fitful, empty hours of the night. In the morning I tuck them away.

Once a day I open the diary Clarice gave me, but fail to put anything down.

In the fragile moments before sleep I speak to Mary, as in times of trouble I've always searched for refuge in the comfort of her love. Except I wonder now if she would accept me. If of all the people in the world she would forgive me for what I did and have done, for killing Baxter, for letting his murder rest inside me these forty years, turning my life into a divided truth. For the distance I've so quickly put between me and my daughter.

The other inmates don't bother me on account of my age and the profound, if misguided, respect they have for my having killed a cop. Some of the first-timers not in for more than three or four years – maybe like I would've been had I gone to jail when I was eighteen – they come to me for advice. Guess they see me with my books and think I have some kind of answers. Guess they think that because of the strange circumstances of my imprisonment I'm privy to certain secrets. Most just want to know how I got away with it. They want the blood and guts of it, but others, they want to know how they might make good for the crimes they've committed. They come to me with the Bible in their hands. What I tell them is that they've come to the wrong man.

On the day of my sentencing, as I'm led through the courthouse, Harrison stops me. 'I think you'll be all right,' he says. 'The DA isn't looking to nail you. He just needs to see some justice done.'

In the courtroom I sit next to my lawyer. Several rows behind me in the mostly empty pews Clarice and Tanya sit side by side, Clarice in a grey, no-nonsense business suit; Tanya in jeans and a plaid shirt that looks like she's taken it from her old man. I saw them when I was brought in. They were holding hands. Before Clarice could make any eye contact with me I turned away. Tanya, though, gave me a look.

The District Attorney is up first and argues that the law cannot allow for the murder of any person, and especially not a police officer, no matter how long ago, to go unpunished. He is asking for a minimum sentence of ten years.

I turn to look at Clarice. She looks at me just quickly, without a smile, a barely contained anxiety pulling on her face, and I wonder what she wishes most at this moment, watching her old man put on the block. That she didn't have to be here? That she didn't have to look at me? That I wasn't her father? The fact is: I killed a man. The fact is: her mother died. The fact is: I'm guilty and being sentenced. These facts don't change.

In his turn my lawyer says that in the course of my life, by being a good and law-abiding citizen, by having educated myself and worked to educate my daughter, by giving her opportunities I never had, I've repaid my debt to society. He is asking for leniency and a humane and practical sentence of probation with community service.

Following this, witnesses are called. The first is my boss from the warehouse, testifying on behalf of my good character. Then someone from the old neighbourhood who remembers Baxter and felt obliged to come up to New York to testify. Then a detective from Dade County, Florida, a young guy. He reads Mrs Wilson's testimony.

Harrison is last. He takes the stand with the weight of experience, walking with sure steps, tugging on the ends of his sports coat to straighten it, raising his right hand. In his opinion, he says, mine was a singular act of violence committed by a frightened young man who didn't know any better. It is his belief I've more than redeemed myself.

As further evidence my lawyer offers the videotape of my confession. I look away. It's like watching someone else. An actor playing my part in a movie. He looks like me and talks like me and moves and acts like me, but he isn't me. Listening to him go on about Baxter – none of it is true. The *facts* are true, yes – Baxter *did* beat me – but the *intention.* What really, in actuality, happened back forty years ago down in Miami is that I wanted to kill Baxter. I could've fought back, taken him down with my fists. I could've run like I ended up doing anyway. But what I wanted was to hurt him. I wanted vengeance, and what I did, I got myself that gun and I waited for Baxter and I shot him. Not once but twice. And for some long minutes in there it felt good to have done it, to have wiped off the face of the earth this man who beat me, and I felt like I didn't care what was going to happen to me, then and for the rest of my life, and for a second I held control over another man's life, his fate, as well as my own, right in the palm of my hands – but the man in the video, looking back at me, using my words, my expressions, he isn't telling this. This is what no one knows. The reason I used to think Mary was taken from me.

I turn again to Clarice. This video is the first she's heard of the details of what I did and I wish suddenly that she'd heard it straight from my mouth and I feel that I've betrayed her, but at the same time I wish she weren't here at all, so as not to hear the story of how Baxter beat me, of how I didn't fight back, of how I shot him. I look at her. As she watches she holds Tanya's hand. Her eyes are fixed on the screen. Once, she looks in my direction.

When the video is over and the judge asks if I want to say anything, my lawyer nudges me and whispers, 'You're up, Nelson. This is it.' Clarice doesn't see me watching her, like you look at your children, like when you watch them sleeping. She's taken Tanya's hand and holds it now in both of hers in a way that reminds me of how Mary held mine in her last days, as if *I* was the one who, in the face of her death, needed courage. As if dying was the easier of the two options.

I stand. 'No, sir,' I say. 'I have nothing to say.'

'Are you sure, Mr Stiles?' the judge comes again. 'This is your right.'

'I know, sir.'

After I sit back down the judge calls a recess. My lawyer shuffles his papers into a folder. The DA offers him a shrug. Outside the courtroom I wait on a bench.

'Why didn't you say anything?' Harrison sits down next to me, an unlit cigarette in his mouth. 'Might make a difference.'

Down the hall I see Clarice and Tanya huddled together. Tanya holds Clarice to her and it looks like Clarice might be crying. I want to go to her. Tell her I'm sorry she didn't hear these things from me, that I doubted her. I turn back to Harrison. What can I say? There is no right and wrong. Just law. And nothing evens out. Mary, she wasn't taken from me as punishment, and the gift of Clarice could just as well have been bestowed on Harrison or that car-jacker as myself. This is who I am: widower, father, murderer, felon.

'The truth is a slippery thing, Detective. I'm sure you know that.'

Harrison nods. He takes the cigarette from his mouth. 'And your daughter?'

Down the hall Clarice has stepped back from Tanya and is biting at her thumbnail. She flashes her eyes at me, then winces. Tanya takes the thumb from Clarice's mouth and looks at it. From her pocket she takes a handkerchief. She winds it around Clarice's thumb. It looks funny like that, the big white thing around her thumb, like something out of a cartoon.

'I suppose she'll draw her own conclusions,' I say. 'That's the most any of us can expect.'

Once the judge steps back into the courtroom it doesn't take long. I stand as he returns with my sentence of two years, including time served, plus two years probation and five thousand hours of community service. As he reads my sentence, I hear Clarice let out a sigh like she's been holding her breath and been punched in the stomach and I turn to see if she's all right, thinking maybe she's fallen and hurt herself or passed out or that Tanya said something – anything, given that a father's imagination is limitless when it comes to his daughter. 'Course, nothing's wrong with her. She's crying and Tanya is holding her in her arms, stroking her hair, telling her everything is OK, it's over.

Court hasn't been adjourned yet and the judge's still talking, saying he thinks it a just sentence, given the unique nature of my case. I have my head turned, though, and I watch as Clarice, that silly handkerchief still around her thumb, kisses Tanya on the lips, just gently, in a gesture as natural to love as love itself is to being alive.

*

When court is finally adjourned my lawyer says something to the DA and shakes his hand. As I'm led out, Harrison catches me on my way to take Clarice in my arms the way I should've months ago.

'He didn't have to do that,' he says. 'He could've let you go.'

'I know,' I say. 'I know.'

What I Can Tell You

My name is Henry Luce Beauchamps; I can tell you this with certainty. I can also tell you that I am forty-nine years old and that I used to be a Professor of Physics at the University of Chicago. Now I wash dishes four days a week at a restaurant up the road here. My doctor calls it reintegration: I am to *reintegrate* myself into society. 'If you're ever going to lead any kind of normal life, Henry, you need to learn to trust yourself,' she explained as we sat in the living room of my house for our weekly meeting, in her hand the manila folder with the details of my case history. 'And if you ever want to get back to physics, well. It's a step.'

I told her, sure, why not? It's not like I had anything to lose. She marked something in the folder and told me she was reducing my medication. Then she said, 'This is good, Henry. This is very good. This is the spirit that will see you through.'

The restaurant where I work is the Olde Colonial Inn up in Manchester. The Inn – poised on a knoll, its rows of gabled windows obscured by thick-trunked oaks, Corinthian

columns holding its roof aloft like the chin of an aristocrat –
looks like it might be an historical landmark, but buildings
like this aren't landmarks in Manchester. The restaurant
itself has no name of its own and isn't large; the most
dinners they'll do in a night is sixty. The dining, though, is
private; the menu renowned; the service four star – the kind
of place where I used to take my wife, Helen, what seems
like a long time ago, and when he was in his teens, where I
took my son Brian now and then: the summer we did his
college tour; the night of his high school graduation; his
birthday.

The head chef, his name is Bill. He is friendly with me and
I have no reason not to like him, I just don't. He'll say hello
and ask me how I am, but what can I tell him that he'll
understand? What? So I tell him I'm just walking.

'Walking?'

'Yes, walking. One step at a time.'

He nods as if he understands. 'Yeah. One step at a time. I
get it.' Now, instead of saying hello, he'll ask, 'Still walking,
Henry?' And I'll answer, 'Still walking, Bill,' but he doesn't
get it. He'll tell me I'm doing a good job, but I know I'm not.
He says it because he feels guilty and wants to encourage me
or maybe because he is afraid of me. When things get going
behind the line he does a lot of yelling and once chased the
hostess from the kitchen into the dining room, screaming
that she was a sorry waste of cerebral matter. He won't yell at
me like that, though. He'll just say, 'Henry, we need you to
move a little bit faster. You gotta keep up.'

In the kitchen they are all younger than I am, Bill and the
other cooks. The pantry boy, Josh, is barely nineteen. He
used to have my job and sometimes he will tell me how to

do it properly, tell me how, say, to mop the floor. 'Henry. Henry.' I'll look up. 'Henry,' he'll say, taking the mop from my hands. 'You gotta squeeze the water from the mop first, then wipe, then rinse and squeeze again. That's how you have to do it.' As if I don't know how to mop the floor. What I want to know is *why*? *Why* is this important?

When he does that I want to tell him something about what *I* know, something about multi-channel searches for physics beyond the standard model in $p\bar{p}$ and e^+e^- collisions; or about the implications of the cosmological relic density from minimal super-gravity – but these things don't mean anything to me any more. They are only words, without context. Like *quark*. *Quark* is a word James Joyce made up. It has nothing to do with physics. It's only a word. A word Murray Gell-Mann, who invented the theory of quantum chromodynamics and applied the name quark, was fond of.

Something else I can tell you is that four years ago I was living in Chicago with Helen and Brian, working on an experiment. I can't remember the name of the lab, but it's well known to anyone with any interest in physics. They have a hadron collider there. I was leading a group of physicists in the search for a super-particle that would support the existence of super-symmetry as the reigning theory of the universe and apparently I was considered by many to be one of the best in the field.

I say apparently because I know this only from what I've read in the clippings I've cut from industry journals and the science pages of major newspapers – as well as *Physics Today*, *Science* and one or two from *Time* and *Newsweek*.

Most of the articles tell of my achievements in physics: a post-doctoral position at MIT; my work there with Samuel Ting on the discovery of the charm quark; a Sloan Fellowship and my appointment as Associate Professor of Physics at Chicago, followed by the Distinguished Young Investigator Award. Then there are the reviews, good and bad, of my first book, *The Search For Meaning And Other Problems of Modern Physics*. A decade later there was another book, *Beyond The Nuclear Age: The Uses of Physics*, which was applauded on the front pages of both the *New York Times Book Review* and the *TLS*. According to the chronology of the articles which I keep organized in a black binder laid open in my living room, it was around then that *Time* and *Newsweek* took a small interest in me. Recently I've tried to find additional information, but it seems news of me petered out about four years ago and the little written since mostly speculates about my sudden disappearance.

Good days I spend scouring what I do have, reading and rereading, searching for clues to who I am, trying to piece together an image in an effort to sink again into the person I once was. It's impossible for me to find any connection, though, and there is so little in which I recognize myself. Whatever pattern may once have governed the order of the clippings has become lost to me.

Bad days I don't bother.

One clipping that I find myself returning to dates back over twenty years, from when I just finished my doctorate. It's a profile in my hometown paper in Connecticut, just two paragraphs saying that I'd attended the local high school, matriculated to Johns Hopkins, then done my graduate work at Princeton. Next to the blurb there is a photo. In it I look like my son, with the thick brow ridge that hangs over our eyes and shadows them and the look of impatience or maybe disdain and the smile that refuses to be completely open. It's not really a likeable face. Though that isn't why I go back to the article. I go back because it says I graduated from Johns Hopkins with a Bachelor of Arts, but that has to be wrong; it would have to be Science. I would've studied physics, I'm sure. Nothing else I own, though, gives me any indication. I've rummaged through all my possessions, still stacked in the attic where Helen put them when she moved us here. Nothing. No diploma, no transcript. In all the articles the only one which mentions my undergraduate years quips that I seemed to prefer beer and women to physics.

Needing to know, I called the Registrar's office at Johns Hopkins pretending to be an interviewer. I didn't want to tell them who I was and ask them my own major; I could see that one getting around. They wouldn't tell me anything over the phone, though, and I couldn't wait to hear by post, so I called my wife. She went silent at my question and in the background I could hear the chatter of the women's group she hosts once a month.

'Helen,' I said. 'Help me out here. It's nothing serious, I just have to know what I studied at Hopkins.'

I imagined Helen straightening her spine, pulling herself together to face the onslaught of emotion my voice so obviously caused. 'Physics, I suppose. I would assume. What else would it be?'

'Do you have my diploma?'

'You threw it out,' Helen said. 'After you graduated. That's what you told me. You said it didn't mean anything.'

'Why the hell would I say that?'

My wife has never been a weak woman, but there are some things that will make her cry and in the silence I could hear her holding it back, the long breaths as if trying to pull her tears in again. 'I'm sorry, Henry. I don't know.'

My wife's name is Helen Clark-Beauchamps and she lives north of New York City, in Westchester Country, where she was raised. We are separated, but not divorced, and once a month she drives the four hours from Scarsdale to Vermont to visit me. She has been doing this for the last year, since I got out of the hospital, though it's just recently I've become aware enough of my surroundings to be able to distinguish her presence in my life – to look forward to her arrival and to miss her when she is gone. Until the last traces of my illness began to recede I didn't even understand she was no longer living in the house or sleeping in the room next to mine. The fragments of that knowledge came to me only in fits and starts, unconnected and without context. That's the way it worked – a single event or moment emerging in parts, if at all, and then only long after the moment had passed. A second to me was the same as an hour or a day or a month. Even now sometimes, despite my medication, I find myself responding to an action which has already taken place, speaking to a ghost or reaching out to shake a hand that is not there. At its worst, when Helen could no longer care for me and had me institutionalized, time almost stopped.

I was in the hospital for two years, though I have no recollection of the hospital or of Helen taking me there or of any events leading up to it. What I know is what Helen has since told me: she had promised herself to keep me at home and to care for me, but it had worn at her emotionally and physically until she could no longer keep her promise. I told her I understood, but despite my best efforts a sense of abandonment, accompanied by resentment, still finds its way into me.

We were sitting on the porch here on the first warm day of the summer, Helen holding my hand and crying as she tried to explain that she hadn't left me; she'd thought I was gone. 'The doctors all said there was nothing else to do.'

I tried to smile, but smiling comes only with great difficulty. 'It's the thing with mental illness,' I told her, 'you're as good as dead, except you're still walking. That's why they say you're afflicted. You're a zombie.'

Helen cringed. 'Don't use that word, Henry. Say, sick.'

'Because a sickness can be healed?'

'Yes. It means there's hope.'

'Hope,' I repeated. It's a word that confuses me still: *hope.* 'What hope is there for the dead?'

Helen tried to explain why she couldn't move back to Vermont now that I was out of the hospital. Most of what she said I'd heard before, in bits and pieces: saying she'd found someone, a nurse, and that it hurt her to see me and that she needed to be by herself; she spoke about going on, and about our son, and about having found a life among her friends, something she could trust. When I'd finally put all the parts together days later I had wanted to tell her, No. Convince her to have faith. But when the words came Helen was no longer there.

Helen said she couldn't take the chance mine was only a temporary remission. 'I'm sorry, Henry. I can't go through all that again, because it's like you said, you've come back from the dead. I can't do that to myself. Maybe some day.'

'Try living with it. I'm afraid to walk down the street. I'm afraid I won't get there.'

'I don't want you to think I ever gave up,' Helen whispered, her eyes down. 'I didn't.'

'Helen.' I touched her face to make her look at me. 'When you visit and you ask how I'm holding up, how I'm feeling, I'm embarrassed. It implies a weakness. An inability to cope with what any normal person should be able to cope with. It's like asking any Joe Schmoe walking leisurely down the sidewalk to the country store on the corner if he thinks he'll be able to make it. Why wouldn't he? Walking isn't difficult. No, it's walking – and I know how to walk. I've been doing it all my life. But if you come up to me, Helen, a man of forty-nine years, walking down the sidewalk to the country store on the corner and asked me if I thought I could make it, I'd have to tell you, I don't know. I don't know if I can make it.'

Helen looked on the verge of breaking. I took her in my arms, said what she'd done made sense to me. As much sense as anything. Every day of my life was a risk and I understood she could not take it. 'I don't have a choice.'

It was Helen who moved us into her family's house here in Vermont after I was put on sabbatical and it was Helen who saw me through the first year and Helen who pulled me from the hospital and Helen who found the nurse and arranged for my doctor to drive from Boston once a week and Helen who finally dismissed the nurse when the doctor told her she thought I should live on my own. And it was

Helen who bought me a car, thinking that way I could go places, maybe to the lakes where she remembered vacationing as a young girl, or to Burlington.

She and Brian planned on driving the car up for Christmas so we could spend the holiday together, but I told her I didn't want to celebrate and didn't want a tree and especially didn't want to exchange gifts.

'Please, Helen. Anything I have to have faith in scares the hell out of me.'

'How about a turkey?' she asked. 'Can we at least have a turkey?' I didn't want that either, but I said, yes, a turkey would be nice. Helen smiled. She'd take care of it, she said. She'd do everything. 'You can sit with your son.'

Brian was in his last year at Georgetown and I was nervous about seeing him. In the days before Christmas I felt myself slipping. I started to meticulously clean and organize the entire house. The compact discs categorized and alphabetized on one shelf, books on another. Stacks of clothes on the living room floor, washed and dried and neatly folded, in piles according to garment and colour. My shoes in a long row with their heels against the back of the couch. The windows polished. The dirt scraped from between the boards of the hard-wood floor. I was wiping the grease from the hinges of the front door when they drove up the driveway in the two cars, Helen in her old Subaru hatchback and Brian in the new Ford. I watched them with the rag in my hand, then turned back to cleaning, unable to stop. If I stopped I knew everything would stop for me. I would disappear.

The car doors opened and shut and I heard footsteps along the path and on the steps to the porch. I heard Helen say my name, then felt her arms around me. She called to Brian and together they led me into the house. I wanted to grasp hold of Helen or take my son's hand but when this thing comes on it's like watching the world from inside the body of a mannequin. I saw everything: my wife hovering; my son with a beard, grown into his size maybe a bit too much, a little overweight, wearing shorts and sneakers in the dead of winter. I wanted to ask him, *Aren't you cold?* I imagined him answering, *Not too cold to grease the hinges of the front door, Dad,* at which I gave a sudden laugh, but that was all there was from me.

When I came out of it my doctor told me Helen and Brian had stayed for two weeks. My doctor had arrived the day after Christmas, when Helen phoned her, and returned when they left. Instead of calling my former nurse she watched me, living in my house until the relapse passed. I asked her why and she smiled. 'Because I'm staking my career on this. It wouldn't look good on my résumé to have let one of this country's best minds sucker himself into thinking he doesn't have a chance.'

When she was confident it had been only an anomalous relapse and I had improved to my previous, stable condition, she returned to Boston. She continued her weekly visits and Helen came up twice a month. Brian called from school. He made me laugh, something he's always been able to do. Hesitantly he asked if I'd be able to make it to his graduation in May. 'I'd really like you to meet everyone down here.'

I told him I'd try. That was as good as I could do.

A month later, wanting to advance my progress, my doctor suggested I get a driver's licence. I was nervous, but was willing to give it a shot. Another step, I thought. The following month she brought up the job washing dishes, said it would be good to start slow during the off season. After our meeting I called Helen and told her I got a job.

'How do you like that, Helen?' I chuckled. 'From particle physicist to dishwasher. Now that's a career move.'

Helen didn't laugh.

A few weeks ago I was in the bar getting myself a soda, and Bill and some of the waiters and the restaurant manager, Mary, were in the dining room talking about how I'd supposedly accosted the young woman who works in the country store in Arlington and how her husband had come after me with a gun. Though that's not at all what happened, it's just something they find easy to believe, I'm sure, because they think I'm crazy.

Every morning of my recovery I've walked to the store to buy an apple, two bananas, the paper, bread, juice and milk and every morning I've looked forward to talking for a few moments to the girl at the register. I find it pleasant listening to her and maybe I am a bit smitten, but mostly her voice keeps me from thinking about myself. One day I mentioned she had a pretty face and a pretty smile and asked if she would care to join me for a bite to eat in the café across the street. She said, 'Sure,' but the next day when I stepped out of the store with my groceries a man was waiting for me on the porch. He said he was the young lady's husband and that I'd better stay away from her or else he'd call the cops and have me sent back where I belonged. For a moment I was flustered, then I said, 'The University of

Chicago, Department of Physics, experimental group, please. I'd appreciate it.'

'Just stay away from her,' he muttered. That's what happened. You tell me if I accosted her.

I still go to the store every morning, but now I don't speak to the woman and she doesn't speak to me. She keeps her eyes down. Recently, though, she did say she was sorry about what had happened.

But Mary, the restaurant manager, who won't stay at night after everyone else has left if I'm still finishing the last of the dishes, said to Bill and the others I just had that look, like at some point I wouldn't be able to control my physical urges. 'And you know he has them,' she said. 'He's a man like any other.' They laughed, but Mary said it wasn't funny. I wanted to step into the dining room and tell her she was flattering herself. I wanted to tell her she couldn't know about my *physical needs.* My needs involved whether I could make it down the stairs, whether I could finish my meal or could sleep through the night for fear that I might wake to find myself forever stopped. My needs, I wanted to tell her, were more important than fucking.

When I came out the group grew silent.

'Still walking, Henry?' Bill asked.

'Still walking, Bill.' To Mary I said, 'Nice dress.' Before slipping behind the service line and into the kitchen I turned and caught her eye and gave her a grin. Let them think what they will.

I'd like to tell you what I can about particle physics.

Particle physics is, in simplest terms, the study of the fundamental constituents and forces of nature in an effort to determine the building blocks of the particles that make up matter, and so, the fundamental forces that drive our universe. The particles in a question – quarks, hadrons, leptons – are of a size too small to be measured by direct observation and as physicists we are left to infer from the examination of the changes in the particles we know to exist what forces act on the particles at the moment of change. Somewhere in there, within the forces we are able to measure, lies the answer.

In order to create and measure these changes in particles, particles are rushed around an accelerator and collided. What is measured after the collision is the energy and the momentum of the myriad resulting particles. From these measurements, and from our knowledge of existing particle theory, the processes of the universe – what it is makes our universe run – are inferred. That's the best we can do.

I'd also like to tell you what exactly happened to me four years ago, but that I can't do. It started as a kind of mood swing, like the kind I'd get into from time to time. Everything around me felt skewed and out of sync. Colours were off, sounds pitched to odd distortions. When I spoke, my words had a hollowness that made it difficult to distinguish them from my thoughts. I couldn't sleep, afraid of spending the middle hours of the night rolling between the sheets, waiting for dawn. That was how it began: little surprises at suddenly finding myself where I was; forgetting appointments; not answering when someone spoke to me; staring for minutes at something no one else could see. And then the delayed responses; the answer to a question I'd been asked an hour earlier; reaching to touch Helen's hand when she'd already moved. I waited for it to pass, as these moods did, like a spell. Every morning I expected it to be gone.

The last week in August Helen and I were to drive Brian to Georgetown. I remember the fear – I didn't trust myself in the car. So far I'd been able to blame my behaviour on my moods or the lack of progress with my experiment or the hassles of administrative bullshit. I had all sorts of explanations. My family had no reason to think something was wrong. In the car, though, I couldn't guarantee I wouldn't sit consumed in myself for the twelve-hour drive. And once there I didn't know if I'd help Brian with his luggage; if I'd see him to his dorm room; if I'd even get out of the car. Would I embrace him? It took everything I had just to hold onto myself.

Early that morning I told Helen there was pressing work on my experiment. I drove west out of the city to Batavia, pushing the car up to a hundred and five. I'd stolen a bottle of scotch left over from a party we'd thrown, but didn't drink any. In my office I paced the room and occasionally looked at the bottle. When the phone rang, I didn't answer. I checked my voice mail; it was Helen, could I spare enough time out of my life to come home and say goodbye to my son. The phone rang again. After that, it was quiet.

Four days later Helen returned. In that time I'd totalled the car, crashing through a guardrail – an accident most easily explained by a sudden lapse into catatonia. Helen didn't know this when she came home and found me on the couch watching television. She said she was embarrassed for me. She would not lie for me, would not defend me to Brian. She walked through the living room and up the stairs to our bedroom. I heard the door slam. Three days later when she asked about the car I told her I'd been drunk, the same thing I'd told the police.

'What's wrong with you? What's going on, Henry? Please tell me.'

'Nothing. Work,' I said. 'Just work.'

'Have you called your son yet? Do you plan on it?'

'I'll call, I'll call.' I waved my hands. 'When I get this figured out, OK. It'll be all right, honey.'

Three months later I was talked to by both the director of the lab and the head of the Physics Department at the university, as well as the Dean of Faculty and the President. They asked about my experiment, my home life. Were Helen and I getting along? They'd heard rumours. I said everything was under control. Against my fiercest arguments it was suggested I take a sabbatical. Relax. Gain perspective. The experiment would run itself.

When I came home with this news Helen suggested I see a doctor. 'Whatever it is, Henry, let someone help you. Sheer force of will won't do it.' But I told her no. I'd ruled my life with my mind and I wouldn't have it scrutinized and savaged by some pseudo-scientific hack. There was nothing a doctor could do for me I couldn't do myself.

'They can give you drugs.'

'No. I'm not taking any drugs.'

'Please don't yell at me, Henry.' Then, her words measured and calm as I continued walking nervous circles around the kitchen, Helen suggested we come here to Vermont, to her parents' vacation house. There was nothing for me in Chicago, she said.

During the first few weeks there was an obvious improvement in my condition. A few days without any bouts of catatonia or amnesia took the fear from me and I was able to sleep again.

It was November. The leaves were all down, it rained a lot. At night Helen and I sat by the fire, talking or reading, sipping wine. Days, we sometimes went to Manchester or Woodstock. After the first snowfall we walked along the river that winds behind the house, its water black against the new snow. I called Brian and told him I was sorry I hadn't seen him off, blaming it on my work. At my request Helen hadn't said anything to him about what had been happening to me, and Brian, according to Helen, had never asked. He said not to worry about it. I knew he was sincere, but still it disturbed me because at the same time as I wanted to protect him from the knowledge of my illness, I wanted to let him into my world. Though it is a world, I think, where no one should ever have to be.

We joked that Helen had brought me to Vermont so I wouldn't look at any pretty girls. 'That's not a problem up here.' Brian chuckled and I liked that we could be at ease like this. He told me a joke: what's the difference between a girl from Vermont and a cow? About thirty pounds and a flannel shirt. In turn I told him the one about how you compliment a Vermonter. Nice tooth.

Looking back on it now, those few weeks were almost ominous in their tranquillity. That ended the day Helen got a call from the postmaster in town. It seems I'd been standing by the pay phone outside the post office for two hours without moving. He'd thought I was talking to someone, but when finally he went outside he saw I only held the receiver in my hand and when he said my name I didn't respond.

What happened that day happened without warning or cause. For two and a half years I remained unresponsive. I wish I could describe to you how I came out of it, but I can't. It was like slowly waking from sleep, passing from one state to another with no apparent boundary, nothing to mark my stepping through; like knowing one has been sleeping only because of the dreams one has had but can't remember.

I also wish I could tell you why this happened – why my brain malfunctioned the way it did at that time and place – but that's not possible either. There is no reason. And if there is anything I've learned, it is that if I'm going to make it on my walk down the sidewalk to the country store I cannot question why this happened. Like everything, it just did.

I don't have to be at work until four and usually get back by eleven or midnight. I like it that way. It fills the loneliness of the night. When I get to the restaurant there are usually stacks of dishes to be cleaned, left over from breakfast – plates smeared with egg and butter; cups of coffee and cream; glasses sticky with juice; pans caked in batter and burned grease. Before I start on them, though, the first thing I do is go into the dining room.

It's a strange sight, an empty dining room, the tables set with white tablecloths, the napkins in a fancy fold between the utensils – spoon, knife, three forks – bread plate left of the forks, empty water glass on the right above the knife and spoon. It's how I think of Heaven – shining white and untouched and empty. I'll imagine the room full with guests; Heaven come alive with souls and spirits. I'll imagine the din and rustle of conversation: arguments and reconciliations; confessions of love and reunions and first meetings and last times; old lovers in idle chatter and young couples fluttering to reveal themselves; families sharing a meal. My family. I'll imagine the wine being presented and opened, the cork laid beside my glass, feeling the end of the cork with my thumb and swishing the wine around my mouth and nodding silently to the waiter, watching him pour for the rest of the table. Only then, having imagined the dining room at the apex of its energy and life, will I start on the dishes.

In the kitchen they listen to the Grateful Dead. When it's slow they talk about what shows they've seen and what tapes of shows they own and what version of 'Bertha' most changed their life. When he hired me Bill even asked if I liked the Dead.

'Great story,' I told him.

During dinner there is jazz on the PA system in the dining room and when things are slow I'll leave the kitchen to stand behind the service line where no one can see me and listen to the music for as long as I can. If one of the waiters or the hostess or Mary comes behind the line I won't look at them. I'll pretend I'm getting some juice or something and listen so hard my head will begin to hurt. Eventually, when I can feel the stares of the waiters, I'll return to the kitchen.

I'm not fast doing the dishes. When it gets busy I can see the exasperation on the faces of everyone. Bill will say,

'You're gonna have to get going there, Henry. You're gonna have to stop walking and start running.' Josh will look disgusted. He'll tell me I have to pull the glass racks when they're full, that I need to periodically empty the silverware tray and run the silverware through, not save it all for the end. Mary won't say anything. She'll just step in, grab a rack and run it through, her eyes on me the whole time.

It's against restaurant etiquette to step into anyone's area like that, but let her, is what I think. Let them all. If there is another thing I've learned it is that shit work like this – labour for no important purpose – dulls the human spirit and lays waste to the soul.

A journalist recently came to visit me. He was from the Bennington paper – a man close to my age, past his wonder years and without anything obvious to show for it, that was the way he put it. He said his name was Frank and that he'd heard a rumour I was in fact Henry Luce Beauchamps, the physicist. I told him I was. He said he'd followed my career. Sports and celebrities didn't interest him much; he preferred chess and the better writers and, of course, science. Especially physics.

'My one son is studying physics, in fact, at UVM,' he said.

'Mine's studying business.' I was glad to share the bewilderments of fatherhood. 'Typical, isn't it?'

Frank nodded. 'I told mine to stay away from journalism.'

'I didn't have to tell mine anything.'

We both chuckled. He said he'd always found physics to be the purest science, more akin to poetry than anything else. 'There's something mystical to it when you think about it.'

'To a certain degree, yes. You can look at it that way.'

He had of course heard about my disappearance. There were rumours and wild speculations and he wondered if he might do a piece on me about what I was doing in Vermont. Against the orders of my doctor, who regulates all my contact with the outside world and has kept my case from the public, and the request of my wife, who thinks it best for me to avoid the work of my past, I let Frank in.

He began by checking facts. When he mentioned Hopkins I asked if he knew what my degree had been in. He probably thought I was testing him. He flipped a page in his notebook and said I'd majored in physics, minored in literature; graduated Magna Cum Laude.

'Thank you,' I said.

He paused for a moment, bit at the end of his pen, then, speaking slowly, asked how long I'd been in Vermont and why I'd come here. I told him I'd come to rest and he asked if, like the writer J. D. Salinger and the chess master Bobby Fischer, I'd become fed up with the labour of my life.

'No,' I said. 'The work is still valid, but it's beyond my current needs just now.'

He asked me what those needs were and I saw he was eyeing the black binder on the coffee table.

'Fundamental needs,' I said. 'Eating, sleeping, walking. What it takes to get by.'

He asked me if I still had contact with the physics community and inquired about the status of the experiment I'd abandoned four years ago. As far as I knew, I said, the experiment was progressing fine without me.

'But will it work without you? Will they find a super-particle?'

'Maybe.' I chose the word carefully.

'You're not certain?'

I told him I wasn't certain of anything.

'And do you think you'll ever return to the experiment? You might have a shot at the Nobel Prize.'

'I don't think so.'

'You don't think you'll have a shot at the Nobel, or you don't think you'll return to physics?' He looked up from his notebook where he'd so far recorded all my answers.

'These are the facts,' I said. 'I suffer from an until now unknown and largely untreatable neurological disorder. It is currently in remission and has been for the last three months. How long it will stay like this, I don't know. And the remission is not total.' Frank had stopped writing in his notebook as I explained my illness. Maybe he thought it was rude or maybe, as I'd like to believe, he understood a little bit of what I was saying and was not embarrassed to hear it from me, Henry Beauchamps, former head of the experimental group at the University of Chicago and a leading figure in the search for the super-particle that could explain the forces of the universe.

'There is no cure,' I said. 'Some drugs do seem to stabilize my condition so I can pretty much lead a normal life. But it's a life I can't really trust.'

'Let me ask you then. If you felt capable, would you go back to physics?'

'In an instant.' I smiled. 'In a furious instant.'

'So, can I ask you?' Frank said. 'And as far as I'm concerned this can be off the record – in those moments that to you are just moments, but may in reality be minutes or hours or days, what is it you feel? What do you think?'

'The same thing you feel and think at any given instant in time, Frank. I don't know.'

A week ago I woke with a sense of optimism, that this day and all the days to come were mine for the making. Instead of buying my usual groceries, I had myself a sandwich from the deli counter at the store. And at the register I asked the young lady, the same one whose husband had supposedly pulled a gun on me, 'How are you today?'

She looked up, then dropped her head again. 'I'm fine. How are you?'

'I am very well, thank you.' I was glad for her question, because when you're genuinely happy in that rare and excited sense of the word, you want to tell everyone in sight. 'I feel like the mountains at dawn, catching the first glimpse of the sun.' It was corny, but true, and this time when she raised her eyes she didn't lower them.

'I'm glad to hear that,' she said. 'I really am.'

'Not as glad as I am.' I gave her my money. 'Please don't take this the wrong way, but you look lovely today. If I were younger and I weren't married . . . But I'm faithful to my wife, you see, and she is the nearest thing to proof of the existence of God in my life.'

'That's a really sweet thing to say. Does she know that?' Handing back my change she let her fingers touch my palm for a moment in a way more comforting than I hope she will ever have to know.

'Soon enough,' I said.

I sat on the porch of the store to eat my sandwich. Across

the street the breeze brushed the tops of the trees against the sky, cloudless but for a puff of white floating over the line of the mountains that marked the distance. I said hello to customers as they came and went and gave a nod to the few faces I recognized passing on the street.

At home I called Brian, but got his answering machine. Helen was out as well. I almost phoned my doctor to tell her I was through with my medication, then decided against it. I showered and shaved off my beard. The next day, I decided, I'd get a haircut, then drive to Scarsdale where I would stay with Helen for a few days – maybe go into the city together, to one of the old jazz clubs where I dragged her when we were young and I used to come up from Princeton. We would go to DC and stay at the Georgetown Inn and attend our son's graduation and then all three of us would have dinner at 1789 the way a family should: share a few bottles of wine; maybe have the stuffed guinea hen, or the game plate of venison, quail and pheasant, or the roasted duck breast. The way it should be. When I was clean and dry I got on the phone. The reservations taken care of, I tossed my pills in the trash.

At work that night it was busier than expected and the restaurant was understaffed. When I got there I didn't stop for my usual reverie in the dining room but headed right to the kitchen and started on the pots and platters and trays left over from brunch. I'd decided nothing would be as it had; I'd work like the demons of Hell were driving me. But as the night wore on I couldn't bring myself to care about pulling racks of glasses, traying up dinner plates, scraping pans. I stopped now and then to catch the sounds from the dining room while the dishes rose in stacks before me until there was no space left for more.

'You gotta move those, Henry,' Bill yelled. 'I got my hands full here. It's time to sprint.'

Mary grabbed a stack of bowls and began to rack them. I took the opportunity to turn off the stereo. 'Jerry's dead,' I said, not to anyone in particular. I saw Bill give a look to the other cooks, but he couldn't do anything, trapped as he was behind the line, a list of orders stacked up in front of him, more rolling out of the printer.

'Where's table eight?' one of the waiters asked.

'Five minutes. Give me five, I'll have it for you,' Bill said.

The waiter sighed, took two salads from the pantry and barrelled out again. I followed him. I stood behind the service line, just listening. When I saw the other waiter come from the bar with a bottle of wine under his arm, three glasses in his hand, I looked around the corner to watch him serve it and I was thrilled to see the room alive like this, the way I'd imagined it, each table an island, the waiters flowing like a current between them.

'Move,' Mary barked as she came from the kitchen with a tray of plates. I let her pass and walked behind the bar where I pretended to get myself a soda.

'Hey, Henry,' the waiter who'd delivered the wine said. 'You can't really be back here when it gets busy like this.'

On her way to the kitchen Mary spotted me. 'You're going to have to get out of here,' she said.

I stayed where I was.

'Henry, move.' Mary turned away and from the kitchen I heard her shout my name before the door closed. After that it's like piecing together a dream. I took a wine glass from the rack, poured myself some of the house red. It was drinkable, though lacking subtlety, I remember thinking, and I looked around for a corkscrew to open one of the better bottles, but I couldn't find one, so instead I took a clean glass and stepped into the dining room. At a table nearby an older couple had just started on their appetizers, an open bottle of red wine between them. I sat in one of the empty chairs and reached for the bottle. I examined the label. Merlot.

'Can we help you?' the man asked.

I poured a little wine into my glass, swirled it around, sniffed, then took the dry, soft liquid into my mouth where I let it linger for a moment under my tongue before swallowing.

'Excuse me, but can we help you?' the man repeated.

The woman began to stand, then sat down.

I poured my glass three fingers from the top and put the bottle back on the table. I held the glass in my hand, ready to drink. I looked at the couple. I wanted to say something. I wanted to explain that I missed my wife and my son and all the things, big and small, of the life that had once been mine. I only wanted to sit for a moment at their table and then I'd leave them be. But my mouth wouldn't work. It wouldn't open to let out the sounds to make the words I wanted them to hear. What I remember then is looking at the couple, the glass still in my hand, and wanting to cry.